Hidden Talent

(Cooper's Extraordinary Season)

Dr. Rosanna Gartley

A Mouse Gate™ Adventure

Mouse Gate Press
1103 Middlecreek
Friendswood, Texas 77546
281-992-3131 TEL   281-482-5390 Fax
www.MouseGate.com

ISBN: 978-1-64883-2147
UPC: 6-43977-42147-0

FIRST EDITION
1   2   3   4   5   6   7   8   9   10

Artwork and fleuron downloaded from Dreamstime.com
© Cloud321500, © Md Shahadat Arman, © Dariusz Kopestynski, © Vladischern,
© Alexander Pokusay, © Ksenyasavva, © Andrii Kuchyk, © Ylivdesign,
© Anastasia Vintovkina, © Faisal Nadeem, © Ekostsov

Dedicated to my grandson, Cooper. His heartfelt care and concern for his friends and family make him a true treasure.

—Grandma Rosie

Acknowledgments

Thanks to my husband, John for all his support, to my publisher, TotalRecall Publications, Inc.

A special thank you to Cooper, who's help in writing this book was immeasurable.

The Book

Cooper's life revolves around hockey. This 12-year-old is captain of his team for good reason. When some bad luck changes everything, his character proves he is an amazing young man on and off the ice.

Chapter 1

Dmytro awoke to hushed sounds coming from the kitchen. It was nearly impossible for anyone in his family to have much privacy, after all, there were five of them living in a small two-bedroom apartment. His living arrangement was no different from most of his friends and relatives. In fact, many of his buddies and a couple of his cousins lived in the same large apartment complex in the city of Kiev in the country of Ukraine.

Although only 11 years old, Dmytro had been forced to mature quicker than most. Ever since Russia had declared war on Ukraine, everyone's thoughts had become more serious, even the children's. Tonight, it wasn't noise that had awakened him but the lack of it. Everything was too quiet. Usually, he would fall asleep to the sound of traffic outside his window but now there was none. During the day, the complex's courtyard would normally be full of activity with parents kicking soccer balls with their kids, pushing toddlers on the swings or supervising children as they played together. The park benches near the large fountain would be filled with grandparents enjoying the sunshine or discussing the price of groceries. Lately, everyone stayed inside afraid to leave the protection of their walls in case shooting started, bombs dropped from the sky or some other hideous sign of war showed itself. So far, the city had seen little destruction but the citizens were aware their city would be a major target.

Dmytro had dozed off in the bedroom he shared with his grandpa and younger sister, Marta. Looking over, he could see her huddled under the blanket sleeping soundly. It was still too early for the grown-ups to go to sleep so he sat up in bed listening intently, trying to hear the discussion in the next room. It was unusual for his parents to keep secrets but by the tone of their hushed voices, it seemed whatever they were saying he wasn't supposed to hear.

Dmytro laid back down while worrying about many things. For now, his parents still went to work each day. But he had heard on their television soon people would be forced to remain at home. His papa worked in a large factory and his Mama worked in a store that sold many things. He and Marta attended school only a few blocks away while grandpa, called gido in Ukrainian, did the daily marketing, and much of the evening meal preparation. Being retired from work, he spent his free hours meeting with other seniors who played dominoes, checkers and chess When would all of this change wondered Dmytro. He never thought he would be sad to stay home from school but now he was scared it would happen. If his parents could not go to work, how would his family have money for food and electricity and how would they keep their apartment warm if they couldn't pay their bills and worst of all what would happen if they couldn't pay their rent? He had never worried or even thought about these things before. All of this was taken care of by his family but now he worried that someday it wouldn't be.

While Dmytro lay in his bed worrying about their future, his parents and Gido were worrying about those very same things. Some of the men at the factory had relatives in the Ukrainian military and word had gotten out that Russian troops were ready to advance very close to Kiev. The city would be a likely target, due to its large population, seat of government, important buildings and structures such as power plants, factories, shipping yards and many other necessary facilities. Unfortunately, the city could be invaded within weeks or sooner.

This information was not lost of Dmytro's father. He knew it was time to get his family out of the country before war was on their doorstep. In the morning, this information would be shared and some difficult decisions would be made.

Chapter 2

Again, Dmytro awoke to noises from the kitchen. The lack of light showed the sun had not yet risen and it was unusual for his parents to be up this early. His gido was still snoring across the room and it looked like Marta had not stirred. The cold of the floor startled him as he walked barefoot to the kitchen. His papa sat at their small table dressed for work while his Mama sat beside him still in her night clothes. Mama had a balled-up tissue in one hand and it was no secret that she had been crying. Immediately, Dmytro wondered if her tears had anything to do with the whispering the night before. His Mama saw him first, "Why are you up so early?"

"I couldn't sleep anymore," Dmytro responded. "Why are you and Papa up already?"

"We had some things to discuss," his father replied.

"I heard whispering last night after I went to bed," Dmytro said in a quivering voice.

"Come here, son," said his father, "we must talk to you and your sister."

"Is it about the war?"

"Yes."

"Have the Russians come?"

"They are getting closer. Too close, it's not safe here anymore." Dmytro had no idea what to say next. He didn't need to worry about answering as his father continued to explain, "You, your sister, Mama and Gido are going to leave for a while."

"Where would we go? What about you?"

"I'll stay here. The army needs many men who can help."

"You mean you will stay and fight?"

"Yes, if they will have me. It is my duty as a Ukrainian. Listen son, we cannot let Putin have our country."

"No, Papa, no!" shouted Dmytro as he threw his arms around his father's neck, crying openly.

"It will be okay, son. There will be lots of men helping in the fight. Besides, I hear the Russians are running out of people and ammunition. We may be able to end this war quickly. Now dry your eyes. I need you to be strong and help your Mama and Gido as much as you can." Dmytro laid his head on his father's shoulders while he sobbed. He knew nothing he could say or do would change the decision and he also knew from that day on his life would never be the same. "Today you and Marta will go to school as always. While you are there, your Mama and I will start making arrangements to get you out of Ukraine."

"Out of the country? Papa! No! Can't we just leave Kiev for a while? Can't we go somewhere in the countryside? I heard the city is the target."

"No son, the Russians are unpredictable, no one knows where they may strike next. It is too risky for you to stay in Ukraine. Many families have been welcomed in Poland, then once there, some have been lucky to be sponsored to peaceful countries. Would you like that? To be able to walk everywhere safely, to be able to play outside and never hear an air raid siren, never hear explosions or see smoke caused by fallen bombs. Those are the things I wish for my family."

Chapter 3

Dmytro held his little sister's hand all the way to school. He didn't think she knew of the changes their parents were making and he was not going to tell her. He didn't know much anyway. Mama and Papa were still figuring it out. He sat in his desk but couldn't concentrate on his teacher or his lessons. What difference did it make, he may never be in this school again. All day, he took long, hard looks at his classroom, the school library, his favorite climbing apparatus in the gym and the faces of his classmates. He even concentrated on Petro, the big boy in his class who had been mean to many of Dmytro's friends. Even the thought of not seeing him anymore made Dmytro sad.

The school bell rang at the end of the day and the children began chattering while they gathered up their belongings. Most were eager to begin the walk home as was Dmytro. As he stood up beside his desk, he noticed his mother and sister standing at the front of the room beside his teacher. Dmytro didn't need to wonder why they were there. It would be about him leaving school. Now it felt real! The conversation with his parents hadn't given him any definite dates but this was proof it would be soon. To be polite, Dmytro knew he was expected to walk to the front of the room and join his family but his legs felt weak, his hands were trembling and tears stung his eyes. His Mama gave him a quick glance and when all the other children had scampered out of the room, his teacher motioned for him to join them. He took a deep breath, picked up his backpack and walked towards the blackboard.

"Your Mama tells me you are going on an adventure," said Mrs. Stotski. Nothing came out of Dmytro's open mouth; he could only nod his head in response. Everyone could see that he was upset and his teacher put her arm around him. "It is going to be okay, Dmytro, you will see. You may be the first family I know making a move but there will be many more. It won't be long before we will get an order to close the school for safety reasons. My own family is thinking about relocating till this is over."

"Many of our neighbors are beginning to make similar plans. So, you see, it won't be long before little remains the same, as we know it, in our apartment building, community and the entire city. To survive the war, we must make difficult changes," expressed Mama.

"All of us, Anna."

"I need you to say good-bye to your teacher Dmytro."

"Good-bye? You mean I can't come back here tomorrow?"

"No, my brave boy, we will be busy packing what we need to take with us because in a few days we are leaving." This was terrible news; he wasn't ready to leave his friends not to mention his father. The tears that had been stinging his eyes could not be held back any longer. They formed glistening rivers down his cheeks, dropping silently on his sweater. Her looked so forlorn that his teacher placed her arms around him burying his face in her shoulder so he would not see the tears that trickled down her own face. Mama and Marta helped Dmytro collect his books and after making promises to keep in touch they walked out of the school he had known for six years not knowing if he would ever return.

Chapter 4

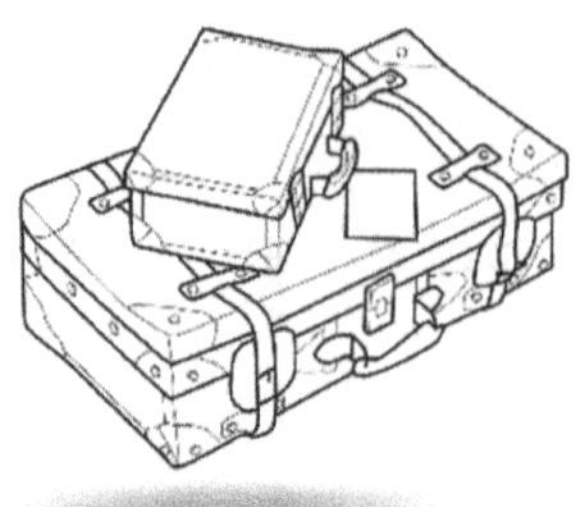

© Cloud321500

The next several days everyone in the family was busy in their apartment. Papa had even taken time off from work to help the family pack up before their journey. Dmytro and his sister were instructed to gather whatever would fit into one suitcase each and their individual backpacks. So, they began the chore of setting out all of their clothing, toys and books. Mama soon joined them and selected the clothing they would need.

"Mama, the clothes are taking up the whole suitcase," complained Marta, "there is no room for my toys."

"I know, sweetheart, you will need many warm clothes as it so early in the spring. You will have to choose just a few of your favorite toys, the rest will have to stay here."

"But Mama," wailed Marta.

"Do what Mama says," replied Gido, "we will soon begin our adventure and we will have much fun." Dmytro knew his grandfather was just as worried as everyone else but he was trying not to upset Marta.

"Maybe we can buy more toys," chimed in Dmytro who was equally as upset as his sister but had a better understanding of the situation.

"We'll see," said Mama glancing a tiny grin at Dmytro. She knew her son was trying to be helpful and she appreciated it. Just as Mama walked out of the bedroom the siren began to wail. It was incredibly loud, a noise no one was used to hearing. Everyone in the house stopped what they were doing, if only for a moment. They had been forced to react to the siren many times in the past and Dmytro felt the familiar lurch in his gut as he and his family made their way to the apartment door. Once in the hallway, they saw many of their neighbors heading to the stairwell also. Although they nodded to each other in recognition, no one took the time to converse. Each family was business only while they herded their loved ones down the many flights of stairs to a safe place in the building's basement. The deafening noise put everyone on high alert. For now, the siren had only alerted the residents of trouble near the city but everyone knew that one day the shrill sound could save their lives. But not today. It was clear that no bombs had hit nearby and eventually the all-clear signal sounded announcing that it was safe for them to return to their homes-at least for now.

"I hate that siren," pouted Marta.

"I know my love. Soon we will hear no more of those and we can relax without worry." Although what Mama said was true, Dmytro noticed his parents did not smile at the prospect. He knew this change was necessary and that his parents felt they had no choice and there was nothing happy about their decision.

"One more night here, Anna. Then you, Gido, and the children will be safe," said Papa. Mama looked around at them all and grabbed Papa's hand. They were both hoping that tomorrow would come without more sirens.

Once back in the apartment, Mama and Papa helped the children finish their packing. Gido had completed his sometime before and was sitting in his favorite chair in the sitting room. He knew soon he would not have a favorite chair so he was determined to make the most of the last few hours. Mama had tucked them into bed earlier than usual, reminding them they would be getting up in the dark and would be on their way to the train station; the first part of their adventure. Dmytro could not fall asleep, he could not bear the thought of leaving behind his friends, his school, his home but most of all his papa.

Chapter 5

A gentle shaking of his shoulder woke up Dmytro. He was surprised he had slept at all and couldn't remember even closing his eyes. He sat up in bed, Gido's bed was already empty and Mama was waking up Marta.

"You two please get dressed now," said Mama, "then come to eat your breakfast." Dmytro dressed quickly and entered the kitchen. The table was set like any other morning. He could smell the coffee brewing like every other morning and his gido was preparing food at the stove like any other morning. Little else was like every other morning. Luggage was piled beside the door as were their coats, hats, scarves and mittens. His parents looked glum and it was easy to see that Mama had been crying and maybe still was.

"Sit children," said Gido, "let's have one last meal together until we will be back here together again."

Marta gave Gido a funny look and said," Aren't we going to eat together on our adventure?"

"Yes, we are, but not all of us are going."

"Who is not going?"

"I must stay behind Marta," explained Papa.

"Do you have to work?"

"In a way. I will join the army so I can help Ukraine against Russia."

A look of terror came over her face and she cried out, "No! Papa! We need you with us!"

"It will be fine. Mama and Gido will take good care of you and Dmytro. I will join you when I can." Helplessly,

Marta looked at Dmytro, then Mama. Dropping her fork, she ran to Papa. He scooped her up in his big strong arms and held her tight against his shoulder. Then Marta wasn't the only one crying. Breakfast hadn't gone well, no one had much of an appetite and it seemed pointless to delay the good-byes any longer. Papa and Gido carried the suitcases down to the car while Mama made sure nothing important had been left behind. The ride to the train station took much less time than Dmytro would have liked. He stared out the car window all the way wanting his brain to take pictures of all the things he was so used to seeing but might not ever see again.

Papa pulled the car into the unloading zone and everyone grabbed the suitcases and backpacks. This time, the good-byes were quick as Papa had to move the car. The tears had all been shed back at the apartment and this good-bye was a mere formality. Papa promised to stay safe and to join the family as soon as possible. They all stood on the curb to watch their car become smaller and smaller. Just before Papa turned the corner out of sight, he gave the horn a couple of quick toots making Dmytro smile despite the ache in his heart and the knot in his stomach.

It seemed odd to Dmytro that the sky was still black with no hint of sunrise. He had been too occupied to think about the time. "What time is it, Mama?" Mama opened her cell phone and said it was just past 2 a.m.

"In the night?" asked Marta.

"That's right. The train to Poland boards during the night. It will be a long ride to get there, about 17 hours. After a quick calculation, Dmytro said, "we won't get there until tomorrow night."

"Right! You figured that out very well, but actually it will be tonight."

"It shouldn't be long until the train arrives here, then we can all have a good sleep while we chug along," advised Mama.

"Where are we going?" asked Marta.

"We will get off the train in Poland where there is no war. The people in Warsaw are happy to have us, to help us stay safe."

"Look children, if you look way down the track you will see the light of the locomotive that is pulling our train." Only for a second, Dmytro forgot about the war and his Papa and looked in awe at the approaching train.

Chapter 6

© Md Shahadat Arman

Several other families boarded the train in Kiev. Even though none of them were familiar to the Boykos, a connection was felt among them. They were all leaving behind what was familiar and on their way to the unknown due to circumstances beyond their control. Their luggage was stowed and the porter showed them to their quarters. For comfort and some privacy, they had booked a small private room with two chairs that turned into single beds. Papa had been determined that his family would have more than just seats in the public car. Gido was quite elderly and Papa knew his father-in-law was accustomed to an afternoon nap. Their trip had begun far too early and would be much more tolerable with comfortable accommodations. The stress from the conditions they had been living through plus the stress of not knowing what the future held was exhausting. But before settling into their roomette, Dmytro and Marta wanted to tour the train so Mama accompanied the children as they made their way from one car to the next. They were all surprised to see that one could eat while on a moving train. The dining car resembled a fancy restaurant with menus and waiters.

"Can we eat here, Mama?"

"Maybe just once Marta. We have brought our own food but maybe we could afford to have a snack in the fancy food car," smiled Mama. Marta's face lit up and it made Mama smile to see her daughter look happy. Although Dmytro hadn't said anything he was also looking forward to sitting on the blue velvet seats of the dining car. Eventually, the train tour came to an end and the four passengers were content to sit in the soft, comfy seats and watch the scenery go by. The excitement of the train ride almost made Dmytro forget about what they had left behind. He stared out the window, watching the sun and its light swallow up the bleak darkness in which their journey had begun. The clickety clack of the steel wheels over the track became like the ticking of a clock- a rhythm that didn't miss a beat nor hint that it would ever stop. Dmytro knew when darkness came again the rhythm would stop and this thought made his tummy hurt. What was waiting for them once they got off the train? They would be in a new country. Would anyone understand them? Would there be food? Where would they sleep? When would he see Papa again? With all the questions and worries it was a wonder that sleep came to him when it did but the very early morning and the reassuring sound of the train soon lulled the boy into a restful sleep.

Dmytro stirred only because someone was gently shaking his shoulder. "Dmytro wake up," Mama called. He opened his eyes unsure where he was for a moment. Mama was smiling down on him and his sister was beside him.

"We have many hours to go yet. How about we have a snack in the dining car?" Mama knew her family would be hungry and she had no idea where they would find food once in Poland. The four of them made their way to the dining car. Dmytro slid into the seat next to the window but was more interested in looking at the menu than the view. As Mama slid in next to him, she picked up a toy that lay beside her son. "Ah I see you brought David."

"I couldn't leave him behind."

"I know my little one, I didn't see you pack him but I'm glad you didn't forget your friend." David had been Dmytro's companion since birth. It was a small stuffed bunny that his baba had made for him. The rabbit had long floppy ears, one yellow and one blue, the colors of the Ukrainian flag. It had been a gift and had been his constant companion until he had been forced to leave David on his bed on his first day of school. There had been many tears when his parents said David had to stay home. David sat on Dmytro's bed during the day and slept with him every night and had gone on every family vacation too. Mama was glad Dmytro felt his little toy was so special. There were few things left from her mother who had loved her grandchildren deeply before she died several years earlier.

"Time to finish eating."

"Then what will we do?" asked Dmytro.

"Well, I brought some playing cards, how about a game or two?" So, for the next several hours the family played cards, walked again through the train and talked amongst themselves. Eventually, they and several of the other passengers met each other and began to visit and compare stories. Gido made himself one of the beds in their room and laid down for a few hours. Mama talked Marta into doing the same ensuring everyone she would wake them when they got close to Poland.

"What will happen when we get to Warsaw?" asked Dmytro.

"I understand there will be some kind people there to meet us. The people of Poland know what is happening in Ukraine and want to help. They will help us figure out a plan," explained Mama. After hearing what Mama had to say he felt better. It seemed that Mama and Gido had planned ahead.

The conductor announced the upcoming stop as the train began to slow down. Dmytro had never been to Poland before and in the dusky light he tried to get a glimpse out of the window of the new country. There were many people waiting on the platform as the train pulled into the station. The Boyko family with their baggage stepped off the train car alongside many others.

"Stay together," warned Mama as she grabbed Marta's hand. Dmytro tucked his hand into Gido's unashamed that he was frightened. A man approached Mama, said a few words, then pointed to a table where several people sat. Mama removed their passports from her bag and motioned for the family to follow her.

Chapter 7

© Dariusz Kopestynski

Dmytro was surprised to hear his mother speaking Polish. "I didn't know she could speak Polish, Gido."

"She can speak some. You had many relatives here. Me, your mother and baba used to visit them often. We learned some of their language each time we came. They haven't lived here for quite a while so I'm afraid your mother and I have forgotten much of what we learned. Maybe you will learn some now."

"Maybe," replied Dmytro, secretly hoping they wouldn't have to stay long enough to learn anything.

It took a while for Mama to fill out papers and for the family to move along to the next table where more papers waited. After a while, Gido, Marta and Dmytro sat down on the wooden platform trying to stay out of the way of the travelers who were coming and going. Marta had dozed off while her head laid in Gido's lap but Dmytro was wide awake. Once the papers were signed where would they go? He soon got his answer. Mama motioned for her family to join her at the last table. She began shaking hands with a man and a woman and everyone was smiling. Could they be some of the relatives that Gido had talked about? Dmytro soon learned they were not but they were there to help. They were the Nowaks and they had volunteered to bring a Ukrainian refugee family into their home. Mr. Nowak nodded to Dmytro and Marta, then spoke to Gido in Ukrainian! That made Dmytro feel better, it seemed language may not be a problem after all. Mr. Nowak welcomed their family to Poland and helped carry their luggage. Mrs. Nowak put her arm around Marta and helped her into the van. Once settled, Mama explained that they would be staying with the Nowaks for a while and that they had one boy Dmytro's age. The drive to their house was quick and Dmytro was glad-he was so tired he couldn't keep his eyes open. Mr. Nowak showed Dmytro to his bed, it was in their son's room who was at the neighbor's awaiting their arrival. Mama and Marta would share a bedroom across the hall, while Gido's bed was in the family's study. Unpacking would wait until morning. Mama quickly found pajamas for the children and tucked them into bed. Closing Marta's door she gave a deep sigh. Now her children would be safe! They would remain in Poland until the next part of their journey unfolded. All she had to worry about was her husband, family and friends who remained in a dangerous war zone. Mama sat at the kitchen table and sent a message to her husband letting him know they were safe in Warsaw and gave him the name and address of the family they were staying with. Mama and Gido said good night to their hosts and made their way to bed.

Chapter 8

Dmytro opened his eyes and was surprised to see it was already light. Back at home, the family was usually up before sunrise. Papa's work started early as did school. Across the room, the other bed was occupied. He could tell from a distance that it was a boy who must have come to bed after Dmytro slept. Pushing back the covers, Dmytro could hear faint voices coming from somewhere in the house. He walked to the door and opened it as quietly as he could. Now the voices were louder and he followed them into a bright, sunny kitchen.

"Ah, good morning," said Gido.

"Good morning," Dmytro replied feeling shy.

"Come, lad," said the man he had met the night before, "come and eat you must be very hungry." He was hungry and took a seat beside his Gido.

"Where is Mama?"

"She is helping Marta."

"Please help yourself to as much as you want. My name is Petro and my wife is Maria. She is outside right now. Did you meet our son, Taras?"

"No," admitted Dmytro, "he is still sleeping."

"Yes, we did not make him get up for school. It's more important that we all spend today together. You can talk about school with your mother." School? Who said anything about going to school in Poland? Was it even possible? Why would he bother to go? Petro saw the look of confusion on Dmytro's face and offered some information. "Our government is making school free and available to those fleeing the war. I believe you would be in the same grade as Taras. It would be a great way for you to meet others your age and make friends." Dmytro hadn't thought of school like that. Making friends sounded cool, trying to learn Polish did not!

Mama and Marta joined them for breakfast. Once the meal was finished and the table cleaned, Petro took Mama and Gido for a ride so they could get acquainted with the neighborhood. He showed them shopping areas, the hospital, parks and the school. Later, Mama shared the information with Dmytro and Marta, explaining that almost everything was within walking distance. She also told them that in the morning, the three of them would walk to the local school to see about enrolling. Dmytro didn't know how Marta felt about going to school but he was feeling a little less anxious. While Mama had been out with Petro, he and Taras had met. Although the language barrier was a problem, they seemed to be able to understand each other using gestures. One thing that wasn't a problem was the video games they settled in to play together. He had decided that Taras might make a good friend. By the time Mama had waved him to bed he and Taras were already comrades!

Chapter 9

The family had been in Poland for several months, routines had been established and they were feeling settled in their new home. Papa was missed but they spoke to him via Facetime every day. He had joined the army and was still learning how to be a soldier. The children went to school daily and Dmytro was surprised that the school day in Poland was nearly the same as in Ukraine. Luckily, his new teacher was fluent in Ukrainian, so at least communicating within the classroom was easy, but doing so on the playground was much harder. None of the children spoke his language but they were eager to get to know the new kid. In fact, Dmytro felt like a celebrity at times. He was usually picked first for any team and was often invited to a classmate's home after school. Marta was experiencing much the same treatment. Other little girls her age were eager to become friends with the new Ukrainian girl. Gido had found that the local park was full of men his age who were looking for a checkers or chess opponent. Gido fit in perfectly. Some of the men even knew a little Ukrainian and those that didn't provided him the opportunity to polish up his Polish! Mama stayed busy in Maria's kitchen. She missed her job but enjoyed having more time to cook and bake. Talking and Facetiming with her husband helped with homesickness. All in all, the family was doing well and had become very fond of their hosts.

Although no one knew how long the Boyko family would stay in Poland, it came as a surprise when one day a phone call for Mama gave her unexpected news. Their family had been placed on a list of refugees who were willing to leave Europe to settle in North America. Far away, in Canada, families who were willing to sponsor a Ukrainian family, placed their name on a list as well. Eventually, the Ukrainian and Canadian lists would be matched. And that is exactly what happened! A family from Saskatchewan, Canada had agreed to sponsor a Ukrainian family that had to flee their home because of war. Mama had only a few days to decide if she would accept the offer. Her first call after receiving the news was, of course, to Papa. Both Papa and Mama googled Canada as well as the town where the sponsors lived. It was a small town called Wynyard that sat in the middle of the Canadian prairies. Its main source of income was farming. Ukraine also had many farms and although Mama had not been raised on a farm, she had relatives who farmed for a living so she was familiar with the way of life. Mama felt she and her family were safe where they were but she also knew they couldn't stay with the Nowaks forever and that they had offered their home because of an emergency situation. They had been very gracious but surely, they would want their house and routine back. Could she move her family so far away from her husband and their many friends and family who were still in Ukraine? It was a huge decision. What was most important? That was an easy question to answer- it was the safety of her children, her father and herself. No doubt they would be safest with the Atlantic Ocean between them and war. Once the decision had been made, Mama felt relieved. Besides, if Canada ended up not being for them, they could always move back to Europe.

Chapter 10

Petro helped Mama navigate the many forms that needed to be filled out before the Boyko family could fly to Canada. Once the paperwork was completed and returned, all the family could do was wait. Part of them wanted to stay in Poland, in the city they had come to know and people they had come to enjoy. However, Canada had issued an invitation and from what they knew it was a large country, filled with people from all lands, many of them having roots in Ukraine. But fear of the unknown was real and they knew that language would be a problem.

It wasn't long before the official phone call was received. They could move to Canada! The news was overwhelming and Mama hung up the phone and sobbed, her hands over her face. Maria soon put her arms around her friend, "It's a dream come true, Anna."

"Is it? Is it a dream to leave Europe, to go to the unknown-a place I've never been?" Maria understood and she didn't know how she would feel if she were in Anna's place.

"You will make the right decision, my friend." Mama told Dmytro and Marta to come in from the yard and explained the phone call she had just received.

"I know this affects us all," she said, "but as the parent, I have made the final decision. I have talked it over with Papa and Gido and decided that we will move to Canada." Up until that moment, Dmytro had hoped they would be chosen to leave Poland but now he was scared. The butterflies he had felt when leaving Ukraine had come back.

"When?"

"Next week. We will fly in a large jet all across Europe and the Atlantic Ocean to Canada. So maybe before we leave, you might want to read a little about flying and learn something about your future new home. This will be quite an adventure!" She had tried to make the trip sound like fun but Dmytro had already had enough adventure in his young life.

Once again, he was forced to say goodbye to friends both in the neighborhood and at school. Once again, he and Marta had to leave what was beginning to feel like home. And once again, the future felt full of uncertainty.

Chapter 11

© Vladischern

The Boyko family had never been to an airport before, let alone been on a jumbo jet. The Nowak family was familiar with the airport in Warsaw and talked Mama and Gido through the steps necessary to board the plane. When the big day came, everyone was excited. The good-byes to friends and neighbors had been made at a party given in their honor days before. This time, saying good-bye had been easier. Now they were off to a new country that they had researched the previous week. They knew their travel plan and who would greet them at the airport in Toronto, then in Saskatoon, Saskatchewan. All of this information made them feel more at ease. Interpreters would be present which was a relief to Mama.

The Warsaw airport was large. The Nowaks parked their vehicle and accompanied the Boyko family into the terminal escorting them to the check-in counter. Mama could understand some of the conversation between the agent and Petro but was very thankful she didn't have to figure out the process on her own. Before going through security, there were many good-bye hugs. Taras and

Dmytro waved a final time as the Boykos rounded the corner to go through security. With their documents in order, the family proceeded to gate 18 where the aircraft to take them to Canada was parked. Dmytro couldn't stop looking out the window. He had never seen anything so large. He was even more surprised when Gido said there would be over 300 people on board. How could anything so big and heavy get off the ground, he wondered. The butterflies were back! As he studied the jet before him, he could see the large maple leaf on the tail and he knew it was one of Canada's symbols. Now he was anxious to board.

Before long, an announcement was made and people started lining up to board the plane. Mama went to the counter to inform them she could not understand the Polish instructions. Many Ukrainians had flown on this same flight before them and the gate agent was familiar Mama's issue. Somehow, she made Mama aware that she understood and after looking at the family's seat assignments, she motioned that she would let them know when it was their turn. Loading hundreds of passengers did not take as long as Dmytro thought. In no time they were seated. He was next to the window and Marta was between he and Mama. Gido sat right across the aisle. The flight attendant helped them settle in and indicated it was time to buckle up. Dmytro heard a loud thud as the cabin door was shut and locked. Then he heard the engines start- wow! They were moving. Take-off was amazing! Sure enough, the gigantic jet lifted off the ground and in minutes the Polish countryside was miles below them. Dmytro could not quit looking out the window. He knew he would remember this the rest of his life. Once they reached cruising altitude, there was no longer much to see out the window. They flew in and out of clouds and the only way to know where they were was to look at the small screen in back of the seat ahead of him. The map showed where they were now and what flight path they would take to Canada. Before long, they were served a meal, the cabin lights were dimmed, it grew dark outside and Dmytro fell fast asleep to the hum of the engines.

Chapter 12

© Alexander Pokusay

Hours later, Mama was shaking his shoulder, "Do you want breakfast?" They were being served more food?

"Yes." answered Dmytro. And sure enough, breakfast was served. He peered out of the window and could no longer see water. Now they were over land. It seemed that he only had time to finish eating and visit the bathroom before the seatbelt sign came on telling everyone to get ready to land in Toronto, Ontario, Canada. Those butterflies flew in his tummy again as he wondered what Canada would be like. Mama had told him that they would only be changing planes in Toronto so they would not be leaving the airport. They would go from the jumbo jet that had taken them across Europe and the ocean to a smaller jet that would fly them from Toronto to Saskatoon. After getting off the plane in Toronto, there was a Ukrainian-speaking airport official stationed at the gate to ensure they found customs and immigration. After showing their documents, they were able to proceed to the proper gate for their next flight. Again, Mama was relieved that the family had help navigating the huge airport.

Getting on the next plane was just as they imagined, only it took much less time to board. Dmytro was getting tired of travelling and he was surprised at how long they had been in the air and still hadn't arrived. "How soon, Mama?"

"We still have several hours to go. Canada is a huge country and it takes many hours to fly across it." Dmytro let out a sigh and went back to looking outside at what was his new country. Soon he dozed off and was awakened by a change in the sound of the engines. He could tell they were going down and it sounded like the engines were slowing. As he looked out of the window, he could make out large areas of green and brown; a river zigzagging across the land and then he saw many houses. This must be Saskatoon! The plane touched down and taxied to the terminal which was very small compared to those in Warsaw or Toronto.

Mama reminded them to look around their seats to make sure they didn't leave anything behind. Dmytro reached for his stuffed David that he had snuggled with on the plane and stuffed it into his backpack. They knew there would be a greeter in the airport and then they would drive two hours to the small town where they would live.

After collecting their baggage, they followed signs guiding them to the main area of the terminal. As they opened the doors, there was a surprise waiting for them. A large group of people with red and white balloons stood bunched together behind a large sign that read, 'welcome to Canada Boyko family' written in both English and Ukrainian. Immediately, Mama began to cry while she placed her arms around her children. Gido did not pause, he walked straight into the crowd, shaking hands and hugging the greeters, despite knowing none of them.

It wasn't difficult for those waiting in the airport to recognize the Ukrainian family. They looked tired, a little apprehensive and unsure as to where to go. A man named Ray, who had grown up in a Ukrainian household knew some of the language and warmly greeted them. He lived in Wynyard and his family had sponsored them. He would be their connection for as long as they needed him. An interpreter explained that the group was made up of some Canadian-Ukrainian families that lived in Saskatoon, some Canadian-Ukrainian families from Wynyard, and some displaced families from Ukraine that had recently been sponsored to Canada. Included in the group, were Canadian well-wishers who had no ties to Ukraine but felt it was the duty of all Canadians to care about those in need. Following the introductions a representative spoke to the family in their native language, explaining that the program he represented was called Solidaire and Open Arms and had organized their flights from Warsaw. He then introduced a Red Cross volunteer who said he would help them get settled once they were in Wynyard and provide further assistance. This was a lot of information but it was provided to make sure the family felt that they were not alone to navigate their new Canadian life.

Chapter 13

Now it was time for the weary Boykos to relax a little during the two-hour drive to Wynyard. With the van loaded, off they went. Even though the new-comers were exhausted from the travelling and the unavoidable anxiety, they could not close their eyes. There was too much to see. As they made their way through the city, Mama was thrilled to see how bright and clean everything was. They were used to seeing destruction and rubble, along with the dirt and dust that followed explosions from miles away. Clear skies and roads were a welcome site. The city enjoyed blue skies, sunshine, decent streets and a calm demeaner. No one was running to a bomb shelter; no cars were dodging huge potholes caused by falling debris. They really were free! She had made the right decision. Her husband would be sleeping now but she would call him soon and tell him all about their journey to the new country.

As much as Dmytro tried to stay awake to take in all the new things he was seeing and hearing, eventually exhaustion took over. He laid his head back and within moments of travelling on the long, straight highway he fell asleep. Marta was already sleeping with her head in Mama's lap and Gido, who was sitting shot gun, looked relaxed.

The slowing down of the vehicle awakened Dmytro. He could see they were approaching a town and only guessed where they were when Ray made a right hand turn off the highway. Very shortly the van turned onto a driveway where a large brown house stood. When they came to a stop, Ray explained as best he could that this was his family's home and they would share a meal together before he would take them to their own house. As they piled out of the van, the door opened and a lady smiling broadly motioned for them to come inside. She pointed to herself and explained that her name was Cindy. Another woman appeared behind Cindy and began speaking in Ukrainian. She was Sophia, Ray and Cindy's neighbor and would act as interpreter. Now Mama could talk! Everyone made the family feel so welcome while they ate an amazing dinner of traditional Ukrainian food and new Canadian dishes.

Following the meal, Ray took Dmytro and Gido on a tour of the farmyard while Anna insisted on helping Cindy and Sophia clean up the kitchen and dining area. Marta was quite happy sitting on the floor playing with the household cat. Their first hours in Canada could not have gone better.

Chapter 14

As twilight approached, Ray, as promised, took them on the short drive into town to the home that had been readied for them. It was best for the family to be introduced to their new home before it was completely dark outside. Ray pulled the van into an alley and proceeded to park the vehicle in front of the garage. The house was blue with white trim. The back door and several windows overlooked the backyard.

Gido exited the vehicle first and began to walk toward the back of the van to retrieve their luggage. Ray proceeded towards the door with a key in his hand and swung the back door wide open. He stood aside on the small deck as Mama anxiously entered their new home. The entrance from the back door opened into an area that had a large closet, washer and dryer. Anna ran her hand over the appliances as she slowly continued into the nearby kitchen. The sight of the kitchen made her gasp and her eyes fill with tears. It was large and modern and bright and spotless. She had never seen such a beautiful work space. The fridge alone was big enough to be in a restaurant she imagined. In the kitchen was also a large oak table that could seat the four of them plus many more. She wanted to stay in the kitchen to explore it further but Ray was leading the way to the next room. It had a beige couch, matching loveseat and two comfy-looking, blue chairs flanked by small side tables. A television hung on one wall but it was the very large windows that looked out onto the street that caught the family's attention. Right across the street was a park! This seemed like heaven on earth declared Marta and Dmytro agreed. Next in the tour were the bedrooms. There were three of them down the hall from the living room. Two of the bedrooms were the same size but one was much larger and had its own bathroom-complete with a tub and separate shower. Yet a second bathroom down the hall brought amazement to them all. Their small apartment in Kiev had been very cramped with everyone sharing the lone bathroom. Each bedroom was also completely furnished. Even the beds had been made with fluffy pillows and cozy blankets.

However, the tour was not finished yet. Ray motioned for the family to follow him down the stairs to the basement. Much to their surprise it was not just a cellar but a beautifully finished, spacious space. A large bedroom, another bathroom and a spacious carpeted sitting area took up most of this level. A door led to a large unfinished room which held the furnace and other machinery as well as many shelves for storage.

By now, Mama was crying again. She could not believe this would be their home. It was more than perfect. Ray made them understand that in the morning they should expect Sophia to visit them to answer any questions they had about the house and to help them get settled. Ray bid them a good night and placed the house keys into Mama's hand where she squeezed them tight. Gido shut and locked the door and watched as Ray got into his van to go home.

Dmytro already knew which bedroom he wanted-the one in the basement! Gido and Marta could have the two in the hall and Mama would have the large one with its own bathroom. He retrieved his suitcase and back pack and made his way down to his bedroom. It took no time for him to place his clothes into the drawers and small closet. He carefully took his stuffed David and placed him on one of his pillows. By the time he got upstairs, it seemed that everyone else had also chosen a room and unpacked what little they had brought. After saying good night to his papa by phone, he kissed Mama good night and for the first time in his life, went to bed in his own room. He loved everything about Canada!

Chapter 15

Dmytro awoke in the dark. The clock next to his bed said it was nearly six o'clock. He had no idea what time he had fallen asleep the night before but it was very early in the morning now. It took a moment for him to remember where he was, but once he realized he was in his own room he smiled and bounced out of bed. He could hear noises above him so he knew someone else was awake. He could smell food, how was that possible? They hadn't bought any groceries. But what he didn't know was that the people of Wynyard along with one of the Canadian agencies had fully stocked the house with everything they would need including groceries. Dmytro began opening cupboard doors and drawers to see what they had when a soft knock was heard at the back door. It was Sophia. She must have guessed the family would be up early. "Good morning Boyko family, how was your first night in Canada?"

"This house is amazing; we are feeling overwhelmed and thankful."

"There is so much more to see. Once you've had your breakfast and are ready, I will tour you around the area," she offered.

"Where will we go?" asked Marta.

"You all need to see the town and the area around it. You kids will soon be signing up for school. You will eventually need to buy more groceries and other things. You will use a bank and the post office too so I will show you where all these places are. I think you will want to see what is outside of the town as well." They sat down to their first meal in Canada. There was much laughter and excitement around the table, then the kitchen was quickly cleaned, everyone dressed and they met back in the kitchen.

"Let's go!" said Dmytro with enthusiasm. So, they all piled into Sophia's vehicle and headed toward main street. The tour was very enlightening for all but what captured Dmytro's interest most was the elementary school. It just so happened that the students were in the playground waiting for the morning bell to ring signaling the beginning of the school day. Seeing the children enjoying themselves made Dmytro realize how much he missed his friends and going to school. "Can Marta and I go to school soon?" Mama looked over at Sophia for guidance.

"I think there will be someone coming to your home soon to explain many things including schooling for the children. But I know the school knows you are coming and are preparing for you. Everyone in town knows about your family and are anxious to get to know all of you," assured Sophia. That made Mama smile. The tour continued and the Boyko family was able to see many things and to begin to learn the English words while Sophia translated.

Just as Sophia had said, a man from an organization dropped by later that day and explained what paperwork would be needed in order to begin receiving grant money, healthcare, a post office box and many other necessities including enrolling the children in school. Soon they would feel that they belonged.

Chapter 16

Several weeks had gone by and the family had met so many people. One of the first places they went on their own was to the Ukrainian Catholic Church. They felt right at home as the priest and many parishioners spoke Ukrainian. Offers came from so many who were willing to accompany them to places where communication was necessary. One of the many places had been the school. An appointment was made and Mama, Dmytro and Marta made their way to meet the school's principal. Although Dmytro was excited he was also nervous as he didn't speak much English yet. After a brief meeting, Marta was escorted to her classroom and Dmytro followed a student to a classroom down the hall. His teacher's name was Mrs. Melsted who had a beautiful smile and kind eyes. All of the children stared at him with curiosity but he clearly looked like any one of them! Dmytro was shown to his desk and before he knew it, the bell sounded meaning it was lunch time. The children seemed to be in a rush to eat then make their way to the playground. One boy hung back, motioning to his friends to go on ahead. The boy was about Dmytro's size, with dark brown hair. He smiled as he walked towards Dmytro's desk.

"Hi," the boy said.

"Hello," responded Dmytro, shyly looking down at his hands.

"My name is Cooper," said the boy as he pointed to himself.

"Hello Cooper, I'm Dmytro."

"Want to come outside and play soccer?" asked Cooper. He understood the word soccer and immediately left his seat with a smile and the two boys scooted out the door to the playground. Play time ended all too soon. When the bell rang the children lined up at the door to walk back to their classrooms. The subject after lunch was math-numbers were the same whether you thought them in English or Ukrainian. Finally, Dmytro could understand!

As the school day ended, Dmytro found out that his teacher was Cooper's mom. Being a teacher, Mrs. Melsted was going to remain after school to coach a team and grade some papers. She gave permission for Cooper to go home with Dmytro for an hour. Dmytro waited for Marta then the three kids walked the few blocks to Dmytro's new home. Mama saw the children coming down the street and was thrilled to see a new friend was coming too. Dmytro explained that Cooper was in his class and that Cooper's mom was their teacher. Somehow, in spite of the language barrier, the three kids had a great time. The hour flew by and Cooper said good-bye to the Boykos. Dmytro was excited to return to school in the morning now that he had made a friend.

Cooper walked back to the school to meet his mom for the ride home. They lived just outside of town on a grain farm, and about 100 of their cows were grazing in a pasture not far away. He had much he wanted to show his new friend. Mrs. Melsted was beginning to put papers into her briefcase when Cooper entered the classroom.

"How was your visit with our new Ukrainian family?"

"It was good. Dmytro has a little sister named Marta. His mom and grandfather came from Ukraine too. But not his dad. He stayed to fight in the war as a soldier. When

Dmytro told me that he got sad and he had tears in his eyes."

"I'm sure they miss him very much and no doubt are worried about him. So many people have already died there. How did you communicate with them?"

"It was kinda hard. They know a couple English words. We drew pictures sometimes; we used our hands to demonstrate and somehow, we figured it out. Then we ate some cookies and milk then went into the back yard and kicked around a soccer ball. That is the same in any language," laughed Cooper.

"You bet it is," said Mrs. Melsted. "It was nice of you to make friends with him Coop. It must be very scary to be here with nothing familiar, especially English. But I have a feeling Dmytro will learn the language quickly. The more he hangs out with you and others, the quicker it will happen. And who knows, you might even pick up some Ukrainian-whether you want to or not!"

Cooper laughed, "Yea, I might learn a few words. Can we have Dmytro come to the farm sometime?"

"Of course we can. You can talk to him at school tomorrow and make some plans. I met with his mom the day before he started school, so she already knows who I am."

"He is really cool, Mom. I think the guys will want to get to know him too."

"We will work on inviting your friends and Dmytro over together sometime when you all have a break from your sports." The ride home from school took less than ten minutes. Cooper's little brother, Oliver and older sister, Dylan were already home. Both were belly up to the table eating some fruit.

"Hey dude, where have you been?" asked Oliver.

"I went to the new guy's house after school while I waited for Mom."

"What new guy?"

"The new guy in my class from Ukraine."

"Oh, that's cool," said Dylan. "what's he like?"

"He seems nice, but he doesn't really speak English. We mainly kicked around a soccer ball in his backyard. Mom says I can invite him here sometime."

"His sister is in my grade but not my class," chimed in Oliver.

"It will take both of them a while to get up to speed- especially with the language. But as I told Cooper, the more you all talk to them, the quicker they will learn."

"I don't think I want to hang around with her," said Oliver.

"I know Ollie, I'm not saying you have to. I realize you have a lot more in common with your guy friends. We've got time for a run before supper. You three change into your running clothes and I'll meet you here in five minutes," said Cooper's mom.

"Hey I know it's too late for this cross-country season, but we should explain to Dmytro about running for next year."

"Good idea, Coop. Just you inviting him to join cross-country will make him feels like he belongs." Cooper wasn't fond of running, but his mom was the cross-country coach and going for a run several times a week wasn't optional. Neither was participating in cross country races each fall. He put up with it because he knew that in the long run it helped him stay in shape for the sport he loved...HOCKEY! Once October came and the arena opened, it was hockey morning, noon and night. All three Melsted kids excelled in the sport and between practices, games and tournaments there wasn't time for much else. In fact, in the winter, the arena was the busiest place in town. If you didn't play hockey, you could play ringette, figure skate or just watch a hockey game.

As the opening of the arena approached, the focus at school turned to the ice. Power skating, figure skating was scheduled as well as free skating. Dmytro soon found out that the arena was the place to be especially on weekends. Cooper had been skating since he was three years old. By now, at the age of 12, skating was no more of an effort than walking or running. He had played his first hockey game at the age of five and had been on a team ever since. He was a natural. Not only did he skate well and stick handle the puck with ease but he had a head for the game. He understood plays and could anticipate what the players on the opposite team would do in many situations. All of these skills made him a valuable member of his team, in fact Coach had made him captain!

Cooper and Dmytro's friendship grew and Dmytro and Gido went to the arena whenever there was a hockey game to watch. They watched the senior men's team all the way down to the little guys who could hardly skate. Dmytro was very familiar with the game. Many good NHL players had come from Ukraine and although Dmytro had never played hockey he had watched some on national television. But now, his favorite team to watch was Cooper's. He knew most of the kids on the team and how he yearned to skate too,

Chapter 17

© Ksenyasavva

It was like someone read Dmytro's mind. One day, when he arrived home from school, a pair of skates sat just inside the back door. He knew they must be for him. Gido was sitting in the living room and he got up when he heard the door open.

"Dmytro, those are for you!" said Gido pointing to the blades. "Ray brought them for you." They weren't new, but they were beautiful.

"Can I try them on?"

"I think you better, but put them on outside, your Mama would not want her floor scratched." Dmytro wasted no time getting them on but they felt a little big. Gido reminded him that many people wear an extra pair of socks to keep their feet warm. With a double pair of socks on, the skates fit just about right. Now he couldn't wait to be able to go to public skating. First things first, he had to tell Cooper about his new skates. Dmytro removed the precious skates and ran downstairs to his room. He gently placed the new footwear in his closet. Racing back up the stairs, he punched the Melsted number on the phone.

Within two rings, Cooper answered.

"Cooper, I got skates!"

"Like real hockey skates?"

"Yes! They were here when I got home from school. They aren't new but they fit good. When can we skate?"

"The next public skate is Sunday afternoon. I don't think I have to do anything else so I will go skating. You want to go?"

"Yes! Yes! I want to skate!"

"I'll ask my mom to pick you up."

"Yes! See you at school tomorrow." At school the next day, Dmytro told anyone who would listen about his new skates. His buddies were happy for him-now he could join in with them on the ice if not the hockey team.

As promised, Mrs. Melsted pulled into the driveway. Dmytro had been waiting and he flew out the door letting it slam behind him with the precious skates in his hand. Outside, the weather wasn't very cold yet but he knew that inside where the ice was it would be chilly so he came prepared with a warm jacket and gloves.

"Hey buddy," yelled Cooper as he opened the car door. Cooper's younger brother, Oliver was also coming along. The new ice arena was on the edge of town and in minutes they were pulling into the parking lot. Dmytro admitted only to himself, that he felt a little nervous. He had a feeling skating was going to be harder than it looked. The car had barely stopped when the doors flew open and three boys made their way running to the heavy steel doors of the arena. Once inside, they saw many familiar faces and managed to find a long bench on which to sit and lace on their skates.

"I'll help you lace them up," offered Cooper's mom, "it can be hard to get the laces tight enough which is important to keep your ankles supported."

"Okay," he answered noticing that many of the kids were getting help from an adult.

"Zip up your jacket, Ollie," reminded Cooper, "and put your gloves on." Dmytro also did what Cooper had said, then he stepped onto the ice. He went to slide his right skate forward when he found himself flat on his butt. Ouch!! Dmytro was both surprised and embarrassed. Getting up was much harder than falling down. In fact, try as hard as he could he kept slipping back down to the ice. Now people were having to skate around the new comer, many of them grinning down at him as they passed. Cooper, wondering where his friend was, turned around to see. He stopped skating and began to laugh. In a moment Cooper was helping his pal up off the ice. "How about you hang onto the boards over there with one hand and you can hang onto me too." This seemed to help. At least he was standing on his blades but instead of gliding forward like everyone else, Dmytro could only take baby steps as the two boys slowly made their way around the ice. What was just as embarrassing as falling down, was that Oliver was speeding around the rink skating at a fast pace and even turning and skating backwards like a pro. He was only a little kid! Dmytro was also well aware that it was his inability to stand up by himself that was keeping Cooper from zooming around the rink forwards and backwards too. Cooper knew he could skate anytime but today his buddy needed his support and he was fine with giving him a skating lesson. After about half an hour Dmytro's feet were sore.

"My feet hurt, Coop."

"Oh, that's because they aren't used to skates. Everybody gets sore feet when they are learning to skate."

"Can we take a break?"

"Sure. Let's go inside and get some hot chocolate."

"I didn't bring any money."

"No worries. My mom gave me some for the three of us." They managed to flag down Oliver to see if he was ready for a break but he shook his head 'no' and whizzed by them with his buddies. Cooper and Dmytro ordered their beverages and sat at a table with a clear view of the ice. They finished their cocoa but Dmytro's feet were too sore to continue. He took off his skates and settled back to watch Cooper making laps around the ice. Some day he would skate like that too.

Chapter 18

Dmytro knew the only way he would get better was to practice. Skating was hard! He wasn't looking forward to putting the skates on again but he knew it was the only way. The arena was used for many groups so public skating was only offered twice per week and Dmytro made sure he was there every time. Mama was working at the local chicken processing plant so she was busy during the day but Gido enjoyed walking to the arena with Dmytro. Many grandparents spent time at the arena watching their grandchildren so it was a great way for Gido to meet those his age. As a bonus, a surprising number of community elders spoke Ukrainian making Gido feel more at home. If Dmytro didn't notice his improvement on skates, Gido certainly did. As the weeks had flown by, Dmytro was skating less and less like a beginner. Maybe he couldn't quite keep up with Cooper or even Oliver but he hadn't fallen for a long time. Not only had Dmytro gone skating whenever he could but he had spent hours watching many of the local hockey teams compete. He was very familiar with the game and yearned to be able to play one day.

Sunday afternoon was public skating and Mrs. Melsted and Dylan were skating by when Dmytro stepped onto the ice. "You are skating so well," praised his teacher. "The last time I saw you skate you were still a little wobbly but look at you now! Soon you will be able to keep up with Cooper's hockey team." Dmytro smiled, he still felt shy around his teacher but was thrilled by what she had said. It only made him more determined to improve. Being good enough to play hockey was all that he thought about while gliding on the ice. The whistle blew signaling public skating was over for the day and Dmytro got ready to walk home. He said good-bye to his buddy Cooper, while Gido, who had stopped by the arena, helped him take his skates off for the walk home.

"Mama, if I get good enough to play hockey, could I?" Mama thought for a moment.

"I'm not sure, I think hockey is expensive. Not only is all the equipment costly but there are fees to join and then the cost of travel to games."

"I think regular hockey is expensive but I heard there is a team that plays for fun. They don't travel much and there are no fees."

"We need to find out more about it. You could ask Cooper and his mom. They probably know about that team."

"I will talk to them tomorrow at school."

Dmytro wasted no time finding Cooper when he got to school the next day. "Hey Coop, do you think I am good enough skater to play hockey?"

"You are getting really fast but you also have to get used to skating with the pads and other equipment on," replied Cooper knowingly. This disheartened Dmytro. He thought he was skating great but he had forgotten what else he would have to wear in a real game. But how hard could it be, he thought. But then he remembered they couldn't afford to buy any equipment.

Once home, Dmytro told Mama and Gido about his hope to play hockey now that he could skate. "Cooper said there are a couple of teams that play just for fun that I could join even though they have already been playing together a while this season." Gido sat quietly at the kitchen table with a cup of coffee listening to the conversation.

"But you would still need a hockey bag and equipment to play on any team," reasoned Mama.

Then Gido chimed in, "I know there is an exchange program here. When kids outgrow their equipment, they donate it to the exchange. Anyone can ask to see what they have and take it if they need it. I think that's where Ray got your skates."

"Where is this equipment?" asked Mama.

"I believe there is a storage room at the rink. You just need to find one of the caretakers. They have the key," replied Gido, who had learned plenty from the other seniors who frequented the arena. Now Dmytro was smiling from ear to ear-he might get to play hockey yet! No one wanted to be part of a hockey team more than Dmytro. He understood that playing the game was much more than skating and scoring goals. He might someday get to play with his best friend, Cooper. That would be a dream come true!

Chapter 19

Before long, it was Dmytro's birthday! He received a hockey stick, hockey tape and a puck from Mama and Marta. But Gido gave him the best gift of all. He had gone through the rink's storage room and had assembled all the used equipment necessary for Dmytro to play hockey. He was so excited he put all his equipment on right there in the living room; except for the skates, Mama said absolutely not!

Dmytro had invited his friends over for birthday cake. Cooper and Oliver were the first to arrive. Both boys were very excited when Dmytro showed them his 'new' hockey equipment. This meant he could play hockey! A knock on the door signaled that more of his friends had arrived. Dmytro sat down to open his gifts and unwrapped more hockey tape, hockey socks, cool skate laces, a hockey net and ball for indoor shooting practice and a Wynyard Monarch jersey just like Cooper's. It even had Boyko written on the back! Now he couldn't wait to hit the ice looking like a real player. It had been an amazing hockey birthday!

The basement's large storage room was the perfect place for Dmytro to practice his hockey shots, at least in bad weather. If they weren't at the arena, Cooper and Dmytro were either at Cooper's farm practicing with Oliver's net or in Dmytro's back yard. Dmytro watched Cooper's stick handling and tried to mimic his shots.

One Saturday morning after practice, Dmytro was taking shooting practice at Cooper's. Mrs. Melsted popped her head out of the door and raised her voice so the boys could hear, "I need you guys to take a break and head to the garden."

Dmytro looked at Cooper, "Why are we going to the garden?"

Cooper laughed, "Because my mom said so."

"But why?"

"It's fall and every year my mom grows a big garden. So now the last of the veggies need to be picked. It has to be done. Every year Oliver, Dylan and I have to help water the garden, pick weeds and help harvest it." This was all new to Dmytro. He had lived in an apartment his whole life. Sure, he knew that someone had to grow the vegetables but he had never really seen them grown. They knew better than to ignore Mrs. Melsted. The sticks were dropped and the boys ran over to the garden.

"Why do you have this wire fence around the garden?"

"If we don't have it up critters will get in and eat the stuff before we can."

"What critters?"

"Deer mostly, but raccoons too." There were a couple shovels and lots of pails waiting for them.

"You guys can dig this row of potatoes, this row of carrots and this short row of beets to start with," instructed Mrs. Melsted in her teacher voice. Cooper picked up the shovel.

"I'll dig them up and you guys can put them in the pails." Sure enough, as Cooper turned over the soil, bunches of light, yellow skinned potatoes appeared.

"WOW I've never seen how potatoes grow before!" Cooper and Oliver just looked at each other not sure if they should believe their buddy or not. Who wouldn't know how potatoes were grown?

"Just wait until we get to the carrots, you won't believe

it!" teased Oliver.

"And if you think the carrots are amazing wait until you find out where steak and hamburgers really come from…and it isn't the grocery store," laughed Cooper.

"Of course, I know where meat comes from," replied Dmytro, not sure if his friends were teasing or not. "Where are the cows?"

"Right now, they are a few miles from here in the pasture but next week my dad will get them into the yard, back there where the barn is," said Cooper pointing to the west. "Then we have to feed them every day because the grass in the pasture won't grow in winter."

"Can I see them when they're here?"

"Sure, I'll let you know when they get here." With three pairs of hands the chore of the garden didn't take long at all. The boys made several trips from the garden to the house with the pails of vegetables. Mrs. Melsted opened the door to inspect their work.

"Good work, boys. I'll put some aside for you to take home, Dmytro. Thank you for helping these guys. Now get back to hockey practice!" she said with a laugh. She didn't have to say it twice, the boys turned right around and ran back to their abandoned sticks. The sun was beginning to set and it was getting cold outside. The boys had almost had enough practice. They were tired and hungry and even Dmytro had to admit he should be getting home. They had had a great afternoon. Cooper even coached Dmytro on how to tape his stick and lace his skates so they wouldn't loosen during a game. Then Cooper told Dmytro something that excited him even more. The town was building an outdoor rink and it wasn't far from the Boyko's home. An outdoor rink meant they could skate even more. It wouldn't matter if the indoor arena ice was being used. Living here was heaven! The following week the boards to the outside rink were erected and the weather cooperated so that ice could be made. The new rink even had lighting so despite the shorter daylight hours, the boys could play for a couple of hours each evening.

It had been dark for an hour and Dmytro's cheeks were more than pink when he came through the door from shooting in the backyard. Gido had their evening meal ready every day when their Mama came home from work. It took him no time to eat and help with the dishes, grab his skates, stick and other necessities for an evening on the ice. Dmytro had been playing on one of the rec teams for several weeks and could already outskate and stick handle everyone on his team. In fact, he wished he had more competition when a coach from another team asked if he wanted to move up and play on a rec team with players several years older.

"Yes, I would!" Now he had a mission. He would practice every day either at the arena or the outdoor rink. He wanted to play on a real team and he would practice twice as hard to make it happen. He told Cooper about his new team and his wish to play on a competitive team. Of course, nothing made Cooper happier than being on the ice himself. So, both boys approached their parents, promising to do their homework and chores if they could get together every evening of the week to practice their skills. Well, maybe not EVERY evening thought Cooper. After all he did have practice and games to play with his own team.

Chapter 20

Cooper, Oliver and nine other hockey-crazy boys converged on the newly built outdoor rink. Someone had thoughtfully placed an old bench just outside the boards. Several boys sat down on it to tie up their skates. Dmytro couldn't wait for his turn on the bench. Instead, he sat atop a small snowbank and began to lace them up. The players quickly divided themselves into two teams, unconcerned that there were no referees. Cooper had brought a couple of pucks while a couple pairs of boots marked where goal posts would be. They were in business! The playing was fast and serious with a couple of arguments but the guys were all friends and knew better than to hold a grudge. It wasn't until Mrs. Melsted drove up to corral her boys that anyone realized how late it was and how cold they felt. Losing two players was signal enough for the game to break up. Dmytro sat on his familiar snowbank to exchange his skates for his boots. He had started walking home when two guys caught up to him from behind. "Hey man, you are skating fast!" said Magnum, "And where did you learn to stick handle like that?"

"I practice as much as I can and Cooper lets me practice with him too."

"You shouldn't be playing on that sucky team," informed Peter.

"Yea, you should be playing with us!" agreed Magnum.

"Thanks, but I think it's too late now and besides my mom can't afford the hockey fees." Magnum and Peter weren't the only kids that thought Dmytro could make their team better. When Cooper got home, he also talked to his dad and mom about Dmytro's skills.

"Dad you should see Dmytro skate and stick handle now. He needs to be on our team," said Cooper.

"Coop's right! Honestly Dad, Dmytro is excellent," added Oliver.

"If you two are praising him he must be good. But I think there are other reasons why he isn't playing competitive hockey."

"Like what else could be the reason. I know he didn't used to be able to skate but now he can."

"Playing hockey isn't cheap, Coop," explained his dad. "I know he has equipment now but there are fees to join minor hockey and not everyone can afford them."

"How much are they?" asked Oliver.

"Well, for the age Cooper and Dmytro are, almost $700.00."

"What?!" exclaimed Oliver.

"Yes, and that's not all it costs. Every time you need your skates sharpened it costs. How many sticks do you think you go through in a season? Each one costs and then there is the hockey tape you put on them. Each time we go out of town to a game we use expensive gas. Tournaments are the most expensive of course. We often have to stay in a hotel and of course buy meals and sometimes there is an entrance fee to be in the tournament. And don't get me started about how much new equipment and skates cost. You guys keep growing so you need some things replaced pretty much every year. We are fortunate that we can afford hockey for you guys." Oliver and Cooper just looked at each other. They had had no idea and felt a little guilty. "But in the end, I think we get more out of being a hockey family than we put into it. Mom and I wouldn't trade you guys being in hockey for anything. But make no mistake it costs money so you can understand why Dmytro can't join. Also, his dad is still in Ukraine. His mom is the only worker here in their family so she can't just skip work or leave early for hockey. His gido doesn't drive so he couldn't take Dmytro to games." The boys went from feeling excited that Dmytro could play hockey so well to feeling sad that he couldn't use his skills on a real team.

Cooper awoke for school with Dmytro on his mind. It seemed unfair that money was so important when all he wanted to do was play hockey. After school, when his team had practice, he was going to tell his team mates about what his dad had said. After all, he was the team captain and he knew the rest of the guys on the hockey team really wanted Dmytro to play with them too. Maybe they could brainstorm together and come up with some ideas.

After practice, the guys were in the dressing room taking off their equipment when Cooper said," I was talking to my dad last night about how good Dmytro is at hockey now."

"Yea, man is he ever a fast skater," commented Magnum.

"I think he should be playing with us," said Cooper. "He is way better than the rec team. He needs to skate with better players so he can get even better."

"You're right," said Coach. "I've seen him skating around the arena at public skating and I watched some of the last rec games he played in. I think the kids on his team are not happy because he scores most of the goals."

"Can't you do something Coach, so he can play with

us?”

"I don't think he could play on this team but I don't see why he couldn't practice with us so he can continue to better his skills. You better watch out though, one of these days he might be better than you knuckleheads," laughed Coach.

"That would be awesome," said Cooper.

"I'll talk to his mom and make sure the idea is okay with her and of course make sure Dmytro actually wants to."

"Oh, he'll want to!" assured Cooper.

"Let's not mention anything to him yet until I talk to Mrs. Boyko," said Coach, wisely.

The following Monday at 5:30 Dmytro proudly walked into the dressing room. He wasn't officially on the team but he could practice with them. His buddies already knew he'd be there. On the day Mama gave permission to Coach, Dmytro couldn't wait to tell the team members. There had been a few bugs to work out. Gido had promised to have their dinner ready early on practice days so Dmytro could eat first before going to the arena. Between Magnum and Peter's parents, he would always have a ride to and from the arena; and Dmytro promised this extra activity would not interfere with his school work and grades.

For the first time, Dmytro glided onto the ice with the team he idolized. The first part of the practice began with skating around the arena to warm up then it was skating and shooting drills. Because Cooper was captain, he had the responsibility of leading the drills for his team. Immediately, Dmytro realized the action was much faster than with his rec team. He actually found himself out of breath in no time, this was hard and he loved it! He had watched Cooper's team play so many games but now being with them on the ice he had a new appreciation for their speed and skill.

At the end of one hour, the boys headed back into the dressing room to change. Every player had a head of wet hair with sweat dripping off their noses-no one more than Dmytro. While his teammates all went home, Dmytro asked to be dropped off at the outdoor rink to practice, practice, practice. If he had needed more motivation to improve, the first official practice session had delivered it. But he knew he would get there. Someday he would be able to match Cooper's quickness on his skates and the strength and accuracy of his shots on goal.

Chapter 21

Dmytro had not missed a game with his rec team nor a practice with Cooper's team. His hockey skills continued to improve and he had become even closer friends with his teammates. One Saturday, just before hitting the ice, Cooper said, "My mom and dad told us last night that we are going to Disneyland for Christmas this year."

"I'd give anything to go there. I've wondered what Disney would be like my whole life," he admitted.

"I didn't know if you even knew what it was," said Cooper.

"Dude! Everyone knows what Disney is. There is a Disneyland in Europe you know, it's in Paris. Some of my school mates have been there."

"Have you?"

"No way. My family could not afford to go. The kids I know that went were rich. I am excited for you. Aren't there two Disney in the USA?"

"Yep, we have been to the one in Florida a couple times but this time we are going to the one in California because my Grandma Rosie and Papa John live pretty close to it."

"What? Your grandparents live near Disney? You are so lucky!"

"I know I can't wait!"

The discussion about Disney came to a halt as the boys made their way onto the ice. As usual, Cooper and Dmytro had a great practice and Cooper again wished Dmytro could play on his team. After practice, Dmytro invited

Cooper to his house to shoot around at the outdoor rink and then stay for supper. It was the weekend and although Oliver had a hockey game in a neighboring town, Cooper decided he would rather hang out with his buddy. Cooper's mom dropped them both off at the house and once Dmytro had put his hockey bag away he couldn't wait to tell Mama, Marta and Gido about Cooper's upcoming trip. Mama knew Dmytro had always wanted to see the castle and ride the rides but it was just a dream.

"How long will your family be gone?" asked Mama.

"I think about two weeks."

"You will have such a good time, Cooper, and I bet your grandparents are looking forward to seeing you."

Cooper turned to Dmytro, "I'll bring you back something from Disney."

"That would be cool," replied Dmytro.

Cooper was getting more and more excited for his trip as the days were marked off the calendar. Before long, his mom began making lists for packing and taking inventory of what they had and what was still needed. Cooper hadn't worn shorts or a bathing suit for months and had no idea where any sun screen might be stashed away. Happily, he hadn't outgrown his summer clothes yet so he didn't have to go shopping, something he hated to do almost as much as going to the dentist. The whole family was excited when the suitcases were brought up from the basement. One was put in Cooper's room with instructions to fill it neatly with the things that were on the list that his mom handed him. Cooper already knew he would pack for himself but his mom would give it one final check before the suitcase was shut for the trip. It was always a little chaotic trying to get everything packed for five people and as usual mom ended up doing most of the packing for Oliver who was good at finding excuses for not being able to do it for himself. Little brothers, thought Cooper.

Finally, the day of the trip arrived. Suitcases were hauled downstairs and placed in the back of their SUV for the two-hour trip to the airport. Cooper looked around the house one last time. The calendar said Christmas was only seven days away yet their house showed few signs of it. They had decided not to put up a Christmas tree as they wouldn't be around to enjoy it. It was also decided, although not by Dylan, Cooper or Oliver, that there would not be any gifts this year. Their trip was to be the gift for all. Cooper saw his cat lounging in his bed and gave him one last cuddle before leaving. His cousin, Alyxa would come over every day while the family was away to feed and play with the kitty. On his way out the door, Cooper grabbed his Monarch hockey hat and jacket. He crawled into the backseat between his brother and sister, excited to get this holiday started!

Chapter 22

Cooper and family landed at the Palm Springs, California airport. He could almost remember being here once before. Of course he had been a little kid then. He remembered visiting Grandma Rosie and Papa John a few years back but, on this visit, he would see for the first time, the house they had bought. He heard their neighborhood had two pools and a hot tub.

They stepped off the plane into beautiful, warm sunshine and Cooper had to remind himself that it was winter. It was even warmer here than on the plane. Cooper peeled off his jacket and flung it over his arm while placing his bulging backpack on his shoulders. It was interesting walking off the plane and strolling outside before coming to the terminal. He stepped onto the escalator and before he reached ground level, he spotted his grandparents and their dog, Molly waiting at arrivals. After all the hugs, baggage loading and settling in it was a quick seven-minute ride to 27 Coble Drive.

Once at the house, the bags were placed in the appropriate rooms then rummaged through until bathing suits were uncovered. Swimsuits were substituted for winter clothes and the happy group made their way to the pool. Over the next few days, everyone was outside more than anywhere else. These days went by quickly and before they knew it the day had come to head to Disneyland. They piled into their rental vehicle and headed to Anaheim. The next couple of days at the magic kingdom were excellent. Cooper had a blast! He rode on countless rides, met dozens of super heroes, although he knew they just wore costumes, and didn't even mind the shopping. He didn't want to waste too much time in the stores but he was interested in bringing home a souvenir for himself and of course one for Dmytro too. The Disney store, called the Emporium, was huge! It seemed to have every imaginable kind of gift one could think of. Aisle by aisle, Cooper carefully checked out the merchandise. He picked out a Disney ball cap for himself. Despite the large selection of goods, he hadn't seen just the right thing for his pal.

On the last afternoon, they headed back to the Emporium. While walking down each aisle, Cooper noticed a jewelry section. He had skipped it the first time in the store but decided to take a look. He finally spotted something that he knew was perfect. It was a chain with a unique medallion.

"What did you find?" asked Dad.

"Look," said Cooper, "first of all it's a small puck but then it has Mickey's head on it that is colored like the Canadian flag."

"Yep, that is just about perfect. Good choice."

"It's even easy to pack," smiled Cooper who had been reminded repeatedly about not buying more than could fit into his suitcase.

It was time to say good-bye to Disneyland and drive back to the desert to the Palm Springs area. Tomorrow afternoon they would head back to the airport to start their journey home, back to winter. But tonight, they would have a nice dinner, enjoy the pool and have one more sleep in southern California.

Chapter 23

Generally, Cooper liked going to school but this morning he was actually excited. He knew his friends would want to hear about his Disney trip and then they would all be together on the ice for hockey practice after school. Time away had been great but he had missed his friends and the ice!

The morning school bell rang and he raced across the playground to line up. When he saw Dmytro crossing the playground from the opposite direction he hollered at him, "Hey Dmytro, you going to practice today?"

"Of course," he answered back.

"After school, my mom can swing by your house to get your equipment and give you a ride to the arena."

"Perfect." School started and ended like it always did. Everyone got a chance to talk about what they did on their Christmas vacation as many of the students had left town during the holidays. No one seemed to mind being back in class and resuming all of their previous activities.

Mrs. Melsted drove both boys to the arena and once in the dressing room, Cooper remembered that he had Dmytro's Disney gift in his pocket. He pulled out the small bag and handed it to his friend. "A snack?" asked Dmytro.

"No, something I brought back from California for you."

"Oh, man! You didn't forget."

"How could I forget you stuck back in Saskatchewan in the cold?" teased Cooper. Dmytro opened the bag and placed the chain and medallion in his palm examining it closely. Cooper wanted to make sure his buddy understood the significance of it so he began to explain, "It's a hockey puck with a mickey mouse head on it and he is painted like the Canadian flag. They had lots of other things to choose from but I thought this one was best."

"It's great! It has three things on it that I like the best, hockey, Disney and Canada. With that Dmytro gave Cooper a fist bump and a high five. Immediately, he placed the chain around his neck. **AND THAT'S WHEN THE MAGIC HAPPENED!**

The boys hustled out onto the ice with the rest of the team. As usual Cooper led his team with laps around the ice surface as a warm up. Everyone noticed that Dmytro was outskating everyone, in fact he was almost lapping some of the guys. Didn't he remember this was just to warm up their muscles before the drills started? Round and round he skated with no signs of being out of breath or slowing down. Next came the skating, stick handling and shooting practice. Again, Dmytro performed the drills to perfection with speed and strength he had never showed before. Everyone noticed it, especially Coach.

"Dmytro, did you do a little practicing over the holidays, buddy?"

"I did lots of practice at the outdoor rink," he confessed.

"It shows. Great job today." Coach was sure hoping this young kid would want to be on his team next year.

"Thanks, Coach." Everyone made their way back to the dressing room to get ready to leave. The boys couldn't believe what they had just witnessed and were eager to find out Dmytro's secret. But there was no secret that he knew of. He had practiced every day and figured it was paying off. But what no one knew was that Disney Magic was working well!

Chapter 24

© Andrii Kuchyk

The hockey season wore on and Dmytro's skills improved beyond most everyone else's on the team. To reward him for his hard work Coach allowed him to sit on the bench during games. He became the stick and water boy. This felt like a promotion and made him feel even more a part of the team. Before long hockey season was more than half over. Dmytro had heard of upcoming playoffs and several annual tournaments. He didn't know if he could travel with the team should they have to stay overnight. He knew hotels were expensive as were restaurant meals. He also knew his Mama worked hard and the family didn't have a lot of money even though Papa sent them money when he could. He would talk to Coach about it.

He didn't have to wait long. Coach explained to the team at the next practice that they had been invited to a tournament a couple hour's drive away. The tournament was just a day tournament, meaning it would start and end in one day. The only expense would be a couple of meals which would likely be rink burgers and fries. Dmytro talked to his Mama about the tournament and she said he could go with the team. He was excited but wasn't sure what to expect. "What's the tournament like?" he asked Cooper.

"Lots of work on the ice but fun too."

"I think we will win," said Dmytro confidently.

Cooper laughed, "We'll see, you never know. We won this tournament last year but the teams change every year."

"So, what happens when we get there?"

"We will be assigned a dressing room, so we put our gear in there. We might not have to get dressed immediately depending on when our first game is. If we don't play right away, we need to watch whoever is playing. We will more than likely play one or both of those teams eventually so we want to learn how they play. I'll be watching to see who their strong and weak players are. if they pass a lot, if they get many penalties, you know whatever I can learn about them to help us win."

"When will we know who we play?"

"Coach will have the schedule. He will likely have a team meeting soon to let us know how the day is set up."

All the players met at the arena. Before they were split up into waiting vehicles, Coach had a short meeting explaining the day's schedule. An excited Dmytro went with Cooper and his parents. The drive went by quickly and in no time they were pulling into the city arena. Dmytro grabbed his skates and helped Cooper with his gear. A sign with an arrow pointed the way to their assigned dressing room. The arena was full of people. They would be playing in front of a large crowd, just the way Cooper liked it. He was excited to play in this tournament which often included several city teams. They were always good because they had so many kids to pick from to make a team. Cooper liked the challenge they provided; he was all too familiar with the teams around Wynyard. He knew his team was pretty strong and would not make it easy for the opposition despite coming from a small town.

They were able to catch the last period of the previous game. Then while the Zamboni cleaned the ice, his team got dressed and as soon as the machine finished its job, the Wynyard Monarchs began their warm up skate. Dmytro joined the rest of the guys on the ice, once again skating faster than most. Even Cooper, at times, had to really push to keep up to his buddy. While skating past the opposition's bench, Dmytro saw a stuffed animal sitting alone. Peter had told him that some teams have mascots. Not like professional sports' teams that had a real, live mascot but a mascot like a stuffed animal or figure. That gave him an idea. Why shouldn't the Monarchs have a mascot too? And he knew just the one! Because Dmytro didn't go far without his stuffed rabbit, he had placed him in his backpack before leaving the house. He raced back to the dressing room. Luckily, the assistant coach was still there and hadn't locked up the room yet. He quickly found what he was looking for and ran back to the bench with David tucked under his arm. He carefully placed him against the glass behind the bench where he could watch all of the action yet not get sat on! Cooper zipped by the bench and saw Dmytro positioning a stuffed rabbit? "What is that? he asked.

"He is mine. I've had David since I was born. I thought he might make a good mascot," said Dmytro, hoping Cooper wouldn't laugh at him or worse make him put the toy away.

"Oh, that's cool. Let's hope he brings us luck and helps

us win." Dmytro breathed a sigh of relief. He knew if Cooper thought it was okay then the other players would too. The whistle blew, sending all the players off the ice, to the bench to begin the game. Instead of making fun of David, every player, starting with Cooper touched one of his ears before stepping out onto the ice for their first shift. Yes! David was a Monarch!

The game ended and the Wynyard team blew away the competition with a score of 12-1. Everyone said the game had been an easy win and it had to be because of the new mascot. The coaches remained in the dressing room following the game. Both couldn't have helped but notice Dmytro skating during the warm up. "Did you see that little bugger skate today?" asked Coach.

"I sure did!" I can't believe how he has improved. I guess some kids are just meant to be on the ice."

"Not only is he fast but he seems to have a head for the game. You can tell he understands plays and can anticipate what the opposition is going to do before they do it. He will be a great addition to the team next year. I'd like to get him into some summer camps. I'm going to start looking for financial help for him."

The Wynyard team won their first two games easily. No one was more excited than Dmytro. He almost felt like he was on the ice with them. The team made it to the gold medal final. Dmytro eagerly watched it unfold from the bench, clutching David for support. With only a minute left and the score tied, a player on the opposing team, desperate to make the winning goal, let a hard slapshot fly. The puck whizzed past the red line, flying flat on the ice and ricocheted off of Cooper's right foot. Cooper immediately collapsed onto the ice in pain. The referee's whistle stopped the play and the coaches made their way to the injured player. With tears streaming down his face, Cooper was helped off the ice to the deafening sound of all players slapping their sticks on the ice and on the boards in support of the injured team captain. Dmytro wanted to bolt to the dressing room to check on his best friend but the game resumed with 38 seconds remaining. No way was Wynyard going to allow them to win now! Magnum took the face-off and immediately shot the puck to Peter. Peter carried it past the opposition's blueline with Magnum close behind him. The goalie anticipated the shot would come from Peter but instead he backhanded the puck to Magnum who let it fly over the goalie's left shoulder and straight into the net. Wynyard won!

Coach entered the dressing room and placed the gold medal around Cooper's neck who managed a weak smile through his tears. By now Mr. and Mrs. Melsted had joined the team and decided to take their son to the local emergency room for evaluation before going home. Mr. Melsted turned to Oliver and Dmytro, "The rest of the team is going to a restaurant for pizza. Do you guys want to go with them or stay here with us and go to the hospital?"

"Stay with Cooper," both boys said in unison.

"Looks like you got a fan club here, Cooper," said Mrs. Melsted, smiling.

"Yea," managed Cooper, still sniffling. Mr. Melsted looked up at Coach and said they would meet the team at the restaurant if possible.

"Okay, buddy, let's get you to the hospital, then we will worry about pizza."

Cooper was helped into the vehicle between Oliver with Dmytro. The hospital was only minutes away and after some initial paperwork, Cooper was taken down the hall to be examined.

Before Cooper could get into the wheelchair, Dmytro handed him David, "Take him he might bring you luck," he insisted. Willing to do whatever might help, Cooper sat David on his knee. The boys watched the wheelchair going down the hall and both of them had their fingers crossed hoping their buddy would be okay.

It wasn't long before a diagnosis was made. The crack was easily seen on Xray and Cooper came walking down the hall with a special boot on his foot. There were no more tears but the glum look on his face said it all. Oliver and Dmytro looked at each other, both understanding the news wasn't good.

"Hi," said Oliver.

"What's wrong?" asked Dmytro.

"Let's head out to the car and we will explain everything," said Mrs. Melsted. "Anyone still hungry?" The boys nodded yes and even Cooper who had been given medication for pain admitted that some pizza would be great. As they headed to the restaurant, Cooper explained what the doctor had said.

"The puck broke a bone on the inside of my foot. I have to wear this whenever I am on my feet to keep everything in place while it heals."

"What about hockey?" squealed Oliver.

"I can't play for about six weeks." The reminder of the diagnosis made Cooper's tears flow again. Everyone felt bad for him. Hockey was everything!

"I'm sorry, buddy," expressed Mr. Melsted, "even the best athletes experience injuries. You did nothing wrong and neither did the player who shot the puck. It was just an unfortunate accident."

"I know Dad, but it doesn't make it feel any better," said Cooper in a loud voice. No one responded. There was nothing that could be said that would make things better.

Chapter 25

Now it was Cooper's turn to be on the players' bench during games. The team had other good players but they certainly missed Cooper. Just at the time when many tournaments were on the schedule and the provincial playoffs were on the horizon, no one knew if Cooper would miss some or all of it. How fast would his foot heal?

Dmytro continued to impress his friends and coaches with his abilities and attitude. Coach wondered if he should approach Dmytro's mother regarding moving her son from the rec team to his competitive team. He had already looked into getting funding for the boy because of his immigrant status. But would he get permission from his family? He would take care of that first before mentioning anything to Dmytro. Coach was already thinking way ahead to developing a team to play for the under 13 provincial title. He had several strong players but with Cooper possibly unable to play, he had to do some strategizing. He knew he would offer players from neighboring towns the chance to try out for the team. He had watched these teams play and had placed their names on a list. To comply with the rules, he had to have at least six players from his own team before he could add others from anywhere else. He could only have a total of 19 players and that included two goalies. He had quite a list of stars from other teams and if he could convince them to come out for tryouts and if they all were as good as they looked, he would add 11 superstars to his own squad. With a stacked team he was almost sure they could win the provincial title.

To put together a team for provincials, Coach knew he had to start soon. At the next practice he spoke to the players about how he would go about recruiting stars for his elite team. He explained that six of them would make the team and that he would need two goalies. He also informed them that he had short-listed 11 players from opposing teams. Out of curiosity, he asked his players if they could pick out opposing players that they thought were good enough to make the team. Sure enough, their names were nearly the same as the ones he had listed, plus a couple more. With that many to choose from he knew he would only keep six from his Wynyard group. He hoped Cooper would be one of them.

Cooper's parents made sure he could be at the arena for every one of his team's practices and games. They knew how important it was for him to feel like he was still part of the team and watched him like a hawk to make sure he always wore his boot when awake. They knew the darn thing was awkward but stressed to Coop that if he followed the doctor's advice, his healing time would be shorter. There was still time for him to be picked for the All-Star team if his foot healed on schedule.

With Coach's new information regarding forming the provincial team, practices appeared to take on a more serious tone. Each player knew Coach was definite about only taking six from their team. They still played as a unit but a sense of competition and a little less comradery was felt among them. Coach's assistant took notes at practice and of course game statistics were very important in making player choices. Everyone was under a microscope.

Dmytro skated as hard as ever. He wasn't focused on

making the new team of course; he was worried about making the Wynyard team next season. As Coach watched him pour his heart and soul onto the ice, a thought occurred to him. Could he somehow make Dmytro be in contention for the All-Star team? First, he would have to get him on the Wynyard team. His mother already allowed him to be on the bench to practice with the team and to accompany them to tournaments. If he could find funding to cover his fees and other expenses, she just might say yes.

The Internet provided all the information Coach needed to find associations that would give Dmytro money. There were many organizations prepared to give grants to children of immigrants. In a few hours, Coach had filled out numerous online forms, shut his computer off and hoped for the best. If enough of the grants came through, Coach would make another trip to see Dmytro's mother with a request that he become a full-fledged player on the Wynyard competitive team.

The grant money was approved so now it was time to speak to Anna. Her English wasn't strong but what he had to say was simple enough. He arranged to visit their home one evening and as expected, Dmytro was at the outdoor rink. Coach presented his case to Anna while Gido sat nearby. Coach was unsure how much the old man understood of the conversation but Anna seemed to comprehend Coach's request. He main concern was the cost of the games as well as how would hockey interfere with her son's studies. After explaining about the newfound money and assuring her that the team's academic performance was always a top priority, she gave her permission. Coach asked Gido and Anna to allow him to tell Dmytro the following day at practice. When the players heard the news, they went wild with excitement. However, each boy had to admit that Dmytro would be a threat to their individual chance to make the new team.

Chapter 26

© Ylivdesign

Dmytro proudly stepped onto the ice wearing his new jersey. He was #10 and he knew it would be his favorite number forever! He had some things to learn. Most of the players had played hockey together since the age of five. His skills were sharp but he had to learn to use those skills while playing with a team. As the weeks went by, David sat on the bench and the team never lost a game. It didn't take long for the newest player to fit in. Dmytro had intently watched so many games from behind the bench and had skated so often with the guys that he had a good knowledge of how to play with them as a team. And it showed as he scored goal after goal.

All Cooper could do was watch. His foot had improved. He was a healthy, young man in great physical shape which was definitely an asset to his ability to heal. His final visit to the orthopedic doctor was scheduled a couple of weeks prior to when Coach would announce his final provincial team picks. He was sitting by himself in the doctor's office after his x-ray. Cooper's dad, who had accompanied him to his appointment, had made a quick run outside to feed the parking meter and coincidentally missed the doctor's final diagnosis. Cooper was back sitting in the waiting room by the time his dad returned.

"Oh, the doc has already read your x-ray?"

"Yep!"

"What was the verdict? I see that boot is off too!"

"Yes, he took it off but he says no skating for a couple weeks yet."

"Really? I thought the last time we were here he said once the boot was off it was back to normal activities," questioned Mr. Melsted.

"I guess, but my foot is still sore where the puck hit it and although the x-ray showed the fracture has healed, I need to take it easy until it isn't sore anymore," explained Cooper.

"Do we need to make a follow-up appointment?" asked Mr. Melsted to the nurse holding Cooper's chart.

"No sir," she answered giving Cooper a big smile and a thumbs up.

"Great! That is great news!" They walked to the car with Cooper limping noticeably.

When they arrived home, mom, Dylan and Oliver were in the kitchen. Dylan was making cookies; Oliver was eating cookies and mom was grading papers.

"Hi guys," said Dad.

"How's Coop?" asked Mom and Dylan in unison.

"Tell them, Coop," said Dad, pointing to his naked foot and leg.

"No more boot!" yelled Mom.

"Back to hockey," said Dylan.

"Well, not so fast, although the bone is..." before his dad could continue, Cooper jumped in,

"I can't play until it isn't sore anymore."

"But then you can't make the All-Star team," explained Oliver, stating the obvious. "You don't even look pissed off."

"Do you think I like it? I don't. But if you had a sore foot like this you would get it."

"Get what?" asked Oliver.

"Get why I don't even want to skate cause it's SORE, you moron!"

"Language, Cooper," scolded Mom.

"I can go to all the games; I'll just be on the bench."

"Of course. Cheering on your team is important too." Cooper acknowledged what his mom said with a shrug and limped into the living room.

"You still have some time before Coach has to finalize the All-Star roster. As long as you can skate by then I think Coach would put you on the team. He knows your abilities and your stats speak for themselves," assured Dad.

"I guess so."

"I wonder if we wrap or tape your foot if it would feel better. A little more support might make quite a difference," suggested mom. "After your shower, I'll wrap it for you." Before bed, his mom wrapped his foot with a special physical therapy tape but Cooper knew it wouldn't make any difference.

Chapter 27

Cooper was at the rink nearly every day and everyday he was asked the same question by at least one person. He was getting tired of telling people about his foot because he gave the same answer every time. It was sore and he was still limping which brought sad looks from his buddies. The days ticked by and Coach's deadline for submitting his final roster from his Wynyard team approached. Once he submitted this list he could start recruiting players from other teams.

"Cooper, dude, what's with the foot these days?" asked Magnum.

"I don't know. It's getting better but when I try a skate on, it feels worse."

"I can't believe you still can't play with us."

"It sucks but I know Coach will have an excellent team. No problem you making the cut. I bet Sam and Ayden from Wadena will too."

"For sure," said Magnum, "and I'll bet Alex and Scott from Foam Lake will too."

"I'll still be there. Just behind the bench."

"Isn't it killing you, dude, that you can't skate?"

"I try not to think about it honestly." Magnum just looked sadly at Cooper and raised his arm for a fist bump.

One day, Coach gathered the team on the ice. I'm cutting practice short today and we are having a meeting in the dressing room before you leave." The players knew what this meant. Coach had made his final decision about which six players to keep. The last drill was completed, the whistle blew and the boys hurried into the dressing room to hear the verdict. Each player had a good idea whose names would be called. There wouldn't be many surprises. Sitting on the wall-lined benches, each player removed their gloves and helmet and began wiping the sweat from their faces. Most already had their skates off when Coach entered the room. The room went silent.

"That was a good practice guys," he began,. "Over the last few weeks, as you all know, each of you have been scrutinized as you have practiced and played games. Your game stats have been monitored but just as important has been your attitude and how much effort you give every time you are on the ice. Having said that, I also want you to know that choosing just six of you was incredibly difficult. This whole team is one of the best I've ever coached. I would want all of you to be my team until you can no longer be in minor hockey. That's how much I enjoy coaching you. So, if your name is not called, I don't want you to think that you aren't valuable as a player. I think all of you are amazing. Okay, let's get on with it." Immediately he called out the names of the six players that everyone knew would be called. Dmytro held onto his Disney medallion as Coach read out the names and then he heard his! Just one important name was left out- Cooper's.

"Thanks for the ride, Coach," said Dmytro as he hauled his equipment out of the box of the truck.

"Anytime, buddy, see you tomorrow at practice." Coach drove off and Dmytro ran to the back door and quickly placed his bag on the basement floor, undoing the zipper to allow it to dry out and to get rid of the stink it released.

Taking two steps at a time, he bounded back up the stairs to the kitchen where Mama was stirring something at the stove. Dmytro came up behind her and flung his arms around her waist. It all happened so fast that she dropped the spoon right into the borscht she was making for supper.

"Dmytro, you scared me!" scolded Mama.

"You're a moron," added Marta.

"You won't think I'm a moron when I tell you I was chosen for the All-Star team!" Dmytro let go of his mother and began jumping and hooting into the living room where Gido sat, giving his grandfather a quick hug as he zoomed by.

"Coach picked you? The team must really suck if you're one of the best," insulted Marta.

"Marta!" warned Mama, "You know that isn't true, your brother plays good hockey. I am proud of you Dmytro."

"I thought I had a good chance. I can keep up with almost any player and I've scored lots of goals since I joined the team."

"I don't know how you do it," said Gido, "skating fast is hard enough but I really don't know how you manage to get it past the goalie like you do."

"I don't know exactly. I just see where I want it to be and I go."

"The games we have been able to watch have been very entertaining," said Mama, "I'm very proud of you. Just remember that this team will practice more and your grades better not change."

"Awe Mama, you know I know that."

"I will be checking with Mrs. Melsted to be sure of it."

"No worries," said Dmytro as he slid onto a chair in front

of a steaming bowl of his favorite meal.

Meanwhile, Cooper had also arrived home from hockey practice to find his siblings at the kitchen table doing their homework. Yes, having a teacher for a mother meant homework could never be avoided.

"Hey Coop. How was practice?" asked Oliver. Everyone in the house knew today was going to be a big day at practice.

"Coach named Wynyard's players for the All-Star team."

"I bet I know who got picked," said Oliver.

"Yep, everyone we talked about."

"Hey buddy," said his mom as she walked towards him and gathered him in her arms for a hug. "I know it's tough that you couldn't be on the team this year. It's just plain bad luck but you'll get 'em next year."

"I know Mom. I get it."

"Knowing you, you'll be playing shinny all summer in the Quonset so you don't get rusty."

"Yea," he responded. Limping upstairs to his room, he laid on the bed staring at the ceiling. He so badly wanted to get his equipment on and be on the ice. Last night he had even dreamt about being back on the team. This was the worst time of his life and it had been his fault. It hardly mattered to think about next year and how he and Dmytro would play together. It was too far away to even imagine it. Cooper didn't know what to do.

Chapter 28

Getting the new team ready for provincials involved changing the practice times. Most of the team was now from out of town and to accommodate them adjustments had to be made. Boys who were used to being opponents were now teammates and it would take some time for them to feel like a team. Cooper could see progress from the bench. This team would be amazing yet he didn't regret his decision at all, well not much. Early on a Saturday morning Cooper work up to a quiet house. Not even Oliver was awake. He crept to the top of the stairs hoping to reach the living room, turn on the TV and watch whatever he wanted for a change before someone else commandeered the remote. He scooted down the stairs and turned the corner to the living room only to see his sister, Dylan already sprawled out on the couch. Cooper began limping but it was too late.

"Uh Cooper, you weren't limping two seconds ago when you were racing from upstairs. What gives?"

"What do you mean? I was so."

"No! You weren't! Why are you lying?"

"Okay, okay," admitted Cooper. "Keep your voice down, no one else needs to know."

"What is going on Coop?" whispered Dylan.

"You know when I went to the doctor a couple weeks ago for my follow up appointment."

"Yes...."

"Well, he said everything was healed and that's why the boot is gone."

"I know that! You told us that!"

"Well, I wasn't honest about the pain."

"What do you mean?"

"I never had any pain after the boot was off."

"Are you kidding? What the hell Coop? Why would you lie about that?"

"I have my reasons."

"You mean you could have been skating and playing hockey all this time?"

"Yes, I could have."

"Okay, now I really don't get it. Hockey is your life, OMG Cooper. Who else knows about this? You would have been a shoe in for the All-Star team and been able to play in provincials!"

"I know, I know. I faked having pain and I faked that the doctor said not to skate because I wanted Dmytro to have a shot at making the team."

"You did this for Dmytro?"

"He deserves it. I could pretty much tell who would make the team from Wynyard and if I was in the running, I knew Dmytro would have less of a chance. But if one of us couldn't be chosen he would have pretty good odds. The way I saw it there were seven of us who were the strongest, but without me there was a group of six." Dylan jumped up off the couch and hugged her brother tight.

"You are the best brother I could think of," she gushed. "That's the nicest thing I have ever heard of someone doing."

"It just seemed the right thing to do," said Cooper modestly. "Please don't tell anyone."

"No, I won't but are you going to keep limping?"

"I think I'll start saying it's feeling better now that Coach has submitted the final roster. I'll do it gradually so no one suspects."

"You are the best."

"Okay, enough already, I gotta eat before hockey practice." Dylan turned back to reading her book while thinking what a great kid her brother was.

Chapter 29

The Wynyard All-Stars had only a few weeks to practice before the provincial tournament. The players were organized and serious while on the ice but the dressing room was always loud with teasing, laughing and fun. Just the way it should be. Cooper was happy to be with the guys and staying off the ice really didn't bother him as it had been his decision. By now, the new team was looking good! The coaches knew they had chosen the right players.

Excitement was growing within the team and the community. It had been said that the under 13 team had a good shot at gold. Even Gido and his fellow seniors who met daily at the rink for coffee and gossip thought the team looked promising.

The first game was in Wynyard and Dmytro had never felt so proud as when he stood on the blue line, his helmet under his arm for the playing of O Canada! While Marta, Mama and Gido stood solemnly for the anthem, Mama stood with tears in her eyes. It was impossible for her not to reflect on how welcoming Canada had been to her family. They had arrived with little money, little English, no friends, no house, no job and now they were rich beyond money. While hearing the national anthem, her tears were ones of joy and gratitude. She was about to watch her son try to win a gold medal in a sport that a year ago he had only watched on television. The music ended and Mama couldn't help but yell, "Go Dmytro, go!"

In the home town players' box, Cooper had filled the water bottles, lined up the spare hockey sticks and placed their mascot, David, on the ledge of the glass. The door between the bench and the ice was opened and before each player stepped onto the ice, they touched one of David's ears for good luck. The team was confident that this match up was very one-sided. Looking at their opponent's' record it seemed they would easily out score them. It was not to be! By the beginning of the third period, Wynyard was down 3-1. The team fought back and with five minutes left in the game, the score was tied. Dmytro had finished playing his shift but pleaded to be put back on the ice. Against his better judgement, Coach gave him the nod and, in a flash, he climbed over the boards onto the ice.

As the buzzer sounded to end regulation time, the score was tied 3-3. Players on both teams were drenched in sweat but no one was ready to give up. The Zamboni chugged its way off the ice, the whistle blew and both teams hit the ice for overtime. It didn't take long for Wynyard to score and win the game. Fans went wild but no one cheered louder than Cooper. His team had won game one of the series. Of course, his family was in the stands cheering the All-Stars and Mrs. Melsted couldn't help but watch Cooper during the excitement and wonder how he could jump around like that with such a sore foot.

"Look at Cooper, his foot doesn't seem to be bothering him right now, yet earlier he was limping."

"I'll bet in all the excitement he forgot all about the pain," explained Dylan.

"Really?"

"Well, you saw how exciting the game was," said Dylan hoping to throw her mom off track.

"Hmm you are pretty quick to come to Coop's defense young lady, what's going on?"

"Geeze, I don't know," said Dylan defensively.

"You are a lousy liar, Dyl".

"Okay, okay, if you promise not to let on that you know what I'm going to tell you."

"Just tell me."

"When Cooper went to the doctor last month and they took off his boot, his foot was fine. He said that the doc told him everything was healed and he could resume all his normal activities. But Cooper pretended he still had pain because he knew if he stayed off the ice, Dmytro would have a better chance to make the All-Star team. And I guess it worked. Don't tell him you know."

"You mean he gave up a sure spot on the team to make room for Dmytro?"

"That's what he told me."

"Wow! I don't even know what to say," said Mom in disbelief.

"Good. Then don't say anything, Mom. This was Cooper's idea and he didn't want anyone to know about it."

"I really want to tell Dad but I won't say a word. This must have been hard on you to keep quiet too."

"No, not really. I am just so impressed that I couldn't spoil it for him. Until now," admitted Dylan.

Chapter 30

© Anastasia Vintovkina

The Wynyard team worked very hard during the next several games. They continued to outplay their opponents until they made it to the provincial final game. If they were to win this one, they would get the gold medal. However, if they lost, there would be another game they would have to play immediately to determine gold and silver.

Once the puck was dropped, the game was a rough one. There were many penalties that caused the All-Stars to lose the all-important game. Now the series was tied 1-1. In half of an hour another game would decide all. Both teams skated off to their respective dressing rooms for a short rest. Cooper had been busy filling players' water bottles and getting towels ready for the sweat-soaked players. Coach managed to give the team a short pep-talk before they heard the referee blow his whistle indicating the teams should go to their benches. The fans who had been lined up at the concession stand to refuel themselves quickly made their way back out to the bleachers surrounding the ice surface. Gido, Marta and Mama were sitting with the other All-Star families a few rows above the players' bench. Mama couldn't resist blowing a kiss to her boy when he glanced up her way.

Both teams were already tired but the thought of the gold medal fueled them on to play another 60 minutes of intense hockey. The battle was fierce, as one team scored, the other team answered back with a goal of their own until with two minutes left in the game that was tied at four apiece. The opposition received a well-deserved penalty for tripping. Now, the All-Stars had a player advantage! It would be now or never. Coach nodded to his first line to get out on the ice. The boys didn't have to be told twice. They leaped over the boards and found their positions. Magnum stick handled the puck around a couple of defensemen, then smoothly shot a pass to Dmytro. Now it was only Dmytro against the goalie. He eyed the top right corner above the goalie's shoulder and slapped the puck with all he had. The goalie barely saw the black streak coming at him and without any time to block the shot, it bounced into the back of the net. When the red light came on indicating a goal, it was the best feeling Dmytro had ever felt.

The crowd went crazy, the All-Star bench vibrated as the players cheered, screamed and hugged each other. But there was still 33 seconds left to play and because of the scored goal, the opposition had all their players back on the ice. Coach signaled to Dmytro to get him to come to the bench for a well-deserved rest but there was no way he was getting off the ice until the final buzzer sounded. And that's what he did. The buzzer sounded and the All-Stars invaded the ice, with whoops, high fives and hugs, giving Dmytro the most slaps on the back and knocks on his helmet.

Both teams lined up to shake hands and then the medal

presentation ceremony began. The opposition received their silver medals first and then the All-Stars placed their gloves, sticks and helmets down on the ice. Mrs. Melsted was as proud of Cooper as if it was him that had scored the winning goal. She couldn't take her eyes off her son. Then she noticed he was holding back tears as the gold medal was placed around Dmytro's neck. She realized she was also crying. They were crying for the same reason; she knew that for sure. The tears were mainly for pride and excitement for the team. But maybe there were a few tears of regret too. Regret that Cooper had missed out on an amazing opportunity to play a game that he loved more than anything else and to win at a high level that would be difficult to repeat. Some of her Mama tears were shed because she was so incredibly proud of her son's kindness and sacrifice toward his friend who had already lived through more horror than most people could imagine. It would be very difficult for her not to let him know that she knew but she would respect his humbleness and cherish it.

Chapter 31

The hockey season for the Wynyard team, was over for another year. The last event was a team family dinner that would be hosted by the Melsted family in their Quonset. There was plenty of food and it was a great time for all the players, their siblings, parents and grandparents to get together and interact in a setting that wasn't the rink. On display, were the trophies and medals the team had won during the season and of course the large, provincial championship trophy made an appearance too. It had been some season!

Once the meal was finished, it was time for speeches. Coach was the first to address everyone. He thanked many people and handed out team gifts to each player. Then Coach explained that the players, at the end of each season, vote on a couple of awards. The most improved player went to Dmytro and the Golden Stick Award, given to the most valuable player, went to Cooper! Both boys walked together toward Coach to receive their awards. The boys posed in their hockey jerseys with their arms around each other's shoulders, smiling broadly as the cameras clicked.

Several parents took control of the microphone to thank various people then an unexpected person slowly walked up to the head table. She held the microphone and shyly introduced herself as Anna, Dmytro's mother. She thanked the coaches, the other parents, the players and the community at large for all the kindness and support her family had received. Then she surprised everyone by saying at the end of the school year, her family would be returning to the Ukraine. This sent the crowd buzzing and Cooper turned to look directly at his friend, Dmytro. When Dmytro finally looked up, his eyes were full of tears for he knew this was his first and last hockey banquet. Everyone clapped when Anna finished speaking but no one was clapping in celebration. For the team and the community, it was sad news. There were so many questions that they wanted answered and no one had more of them than Cooper.

The gathering ended and parents and players began cleaning up. Cooper wasn't interested in emptying tables of plates and leftovers, instead, he made a beeline to Dmytro who was already surrounded.

"Why are you going back?" demanded Cooper, his eyes full of tears ready to spill.

"Mama says life is too hard without Papa, she misses him."

"Can't you talk her out of it, dude," Cooper insisted. Dmytro just sadly shook his head.

"I've tried, Coop, but her mind is made up."

"Then let them go back but you stay here. Maybe my parents would let you move in with us." Even as Cooper said it, he knew it sounded crazy. He couldn't live in a different country without his family.

"No, I miss my Papa too. But we aren't leaving until school ends. So, I will be here for a while longer." That did not help Cooper feel better. Dmytro was his best friend and next year they would have played hockey together for the first time. Cooper couldn't ask for a better team mate but now it was all crashing down.

"But we need you on the team," pleaded Cooper, "you

and me on the same team, dude, no one could stop us.”

"I will miss hockey but I'm going to ask if I can play in the Ukraine." Cooper had run out of things to say. Anna stood a short distance away not wanting to interrupt the boys' conversation but now it was time to head home. On the way out they stopped to thank Cooper's parents and to say good night to a few others. Just before walking out the door, Dmytro turned back to look at Cooper who was watching them leave. Both boys knew their lives would never be the same.

Chapter 32

It was spring, the ice surface at the arena and the outdoor rink would be melted until fall. Cooper's hockey bag rested on the basement floor. It would be there until it was time for summertime hockey school. Baseball sign-ups were at the end of the week and Cooper was looking forward to being on the team. Although Dmytro might not be around to play till the end of the season, Anna would not stop him from signing up too. He needed to be with his friends as long as possible. Spring soccer was also offered and most of the hockey team had joined, including Cooper and Dmytro. The local golf course was close to opening for the season and although Dmytro had never played the game, Cooper was going to give his buddy lessons. Between playing all the sports, it almost seemed like life was back to normal except Cooper's gut knew better. Every day when he woke up, he felt sadness in the pit of his stomach and it stayed right there until he fell asleep each night. The sadness grew deeper as the days ticked by. Usually, Cooper looked forward to the end of the school year-what kid didn't? But this year it meant saying good-bye.

"Cooper, I know you will miss Dmytro but you can still keep in touch. Ukraine has technology just like Canada so you can text and Facetime."

"I know, Mom."

"And who knows maybe sometime we can go to the Ukraine or Dmytro can come here for a visit. You never know."

"Yea," agreed Cooper, halfheartedly.

The last day of school was only a day away. Mrs. Melsted and Coop, Dyl and Oliver had promised Anna they would come by after school to help them finish packing. Their flight was only a few days away. Cooper found Dmytro in his bedroom with boxes scattered on the floor. They would only take their personal belongings back to Ukraine, happy to leave everything else for another family who may need help. Cooper sat on the bed next to his friend.

"Cooper, would you take my hockey bag and equipment to the arena and donate it?"

"You're not taking it with you?"

"No, I'm just going to take my jersey. I won't be able to play in Ukraine until the war ends and by then I might have outgrown my skates and stuff." Cooper had to admit that sounded logical. He had outgrown many sets of hockey equipment over the years.

Chapter 33

© Faisal Nadeem

Several families made the two-hour drive to the city to accompany the Boykos. Everyone had a final meal together in a restaurant before driving to the airport. Most of the families said their good-byes outside the terminal building but the Melsteds stayed until the Boykos had to go through security. Final hugs were given amid tears and sniffles, then it was time for a final glimpse as they stepped onto the escalator heading to their gate.

On the plane, seated between Mama and Marta, Dmytro removed the chain and Disney pendant from around his neck. He took a good look at it then put it back on. Looking out the window, brought back memories of his last time on a plane when he was first landing in Canada. He had been so scared, but it had turned out great! He had learned to skate, made many friends, spent hours at the arena and froze his cheeks while he skated at the outdoor rink. He remembered being given his skates and hockey equipment and then his jersey with the number 10 on it. Of course, his favorite memory would always be winning the gold medal while being part of a real hockey team. Mama looked over at him and commented, "You are smiling, I like to see that."

"I am remembering all the cool stuff I did in Canada."

"Like playing hockey?"

"Yes, and winning the medal."

"It has been an exceptional year, my boy. You will have so much to tell your friends in Kiev." Anna thought back about her year too. Eventually, word had gotten out- because secrets were hard to keep- that Cooper could have been on the All-Star team but instead gave up his chance to Dmytro. Some didn't believe the story to be true but Anna did. While on the plane, she spoke about the story she had heard. Dmytro's first instinct was to text Cooper and ask him if it was true. But Mama placed her hand over his reminding him that Cooper had not revealed his plan to him for a reason and perhaps it was best to keep the secret to himself. This gave Dmytro much to think about and made him miss his buddy more

Cooper had been registered for hockey school months before and this afternoon he and his dad would drive to the city for the first session.

"You need to go downstairs and grab your hockey equipment," instructed Dad. "We need to make sure all your equipment is there and still fits you." Cooper dragged his bag up the stairs and dumped its contents onto the kitchen floor. Besides the usual, out fell a blue and yellow stuffed bunny. It was David with a note attached to him that read, 'Make sure David sits on the bench next season- you can't win without him!' Cooper gave a laugh! "For sure, Dmytro, for sure, buddy."

Title: *Beads of Courage®*
 (Oliver's Story)

- Author: Dr. Rosanna Gartley
- Publisher: TotalRecall Publications, Inc.
- Paper Back: ISBN: 9781590952269
- eBook: ISBN: 9781590952320
- Number of pages in the finished book: 64
- Publication Date: April 25, 2017

Baby Oliver's life started out precariously in the neonatal intensive care unit. Each day, while he was a patient, his parents were given beads of various shapes and colors. Each bead symbolized a medical procedure that Oliver had endured on that day. By the time Oliver was discharged, his collection of beads was impressive.

As Oliver grew, his Beads of Courage® continued to hang on his bedroom wall. Not only were they a reminder of what he had lived through but also served as an inspiration for future challenges.

You won't want to miss what happens during a family vacation when this amazing little boy employs Disney Magic to help those who need a little courage.

Title: *Castaway Crown*
(Matthew and Anna's Undersea Adventure)
- Author: Dr. Rosanna Gartley
- Publisher: TotalRecall Publications, Inc.
- Paper Back: ISBN: 9781590953327
- eBook: ISBN: 9781590953358
- Number of pages in the finished book: 74
- Publication Date: April 25, 2017

Matthew and Anna are full of excitement when they learn their family is going on a Disney cruise. With the magic of Disney both children are propelled into an adventure far below the ocean as they are asked to help the sea creatures get rid of a bothersome ghost. With Matthew's above average intellect coupled with Anna's amazing drawing abilities they solve the two-hundred-year-old mystery bringing peace to the sea and the ghost.

Title: *Oh, Brother!*
   (Emily's Adventure)
- Author: Dr. Rosanna Gartley
- Publisher: MouseGate.com
- Paper Back: ISBN: 9781590953990
- eBook: ISBN: 9781590954003
- Number of pages in the finished book: 70
- Publication Date: October, 28 2017

Emily, an only child adored by her parents, finds her life turned upside down and backyards when her parents welcome into their home, Adam, a foster child. Mayhem, mystery and adventure ensue following an enchanted experience that begins during a family vacation to the Magic Kingdom. Disney Magic enables Emily to visit the past and the future, allowing her to choose a path altering the lives of her loved ones.

Title: *The Quill Lakes' Catastrophe (Ayden's Adventure)*

- Author: Dr. Rosanna Gartley
- Publisher: MouseGate.com
- Paper Back: ISBN: 9781590953549
- eBook: ISBN: 9781590953556
- Number of pages in the finished book: 92
- Publication Date: March 6, 2018

Eleven-year-old Ayden has lived on a farm near the Quill Lakes all his life. When the lakes' flooding puts his family at risk of losing their livelihood and way of life, something must be done. Ayden connects with some uniquely talented forest creatures, uses an ample dose of Disney Magic and relies on his own ingenuity to solve his community's water-logged problem.

Title: *Itchy Feet*
  (Miranda and Riley's Adventure)
- Author: Dr. Rosanna Gartley
- Publisher: MouseGate.com
- Paper Back: ISBN: 9781590952603
- eBook: ISBN: 9781590952771
- Number of pages in the finished book: 125
- Publication Date: April, 2018

Sisters, Riley and Miranda are beyond excited to tour Disneyland, California. While they are enchanted with the attraction It's A Small World, Disney Magic cocoons them transporting the girls back to the time of American slavery. In the woods near their home, the pair stumble upon an unusual campsite and place their own needs and safety aside to help the humble family they have discovered. Because of the sisters' loving hearts and generosity, combined with a healthy dose of Disney Magic, the Birdsong family finds its way to freedom.

Title: *Curve Balls*
 (Sam's Adventure)

- Author: Dr. Rosanna Gartley
- Publisher: MouseGate.com
- Paper Back: ISBN: 9781648831683
- eBook: ISBN: 9781648831690
- Number of pages in the finished book: 96
- Publication Date: May 2022

Sam and his family enjoy a vacation to Disney World where he is thrilled to experience a new ride, The Dino-Soar. This 10- year- old has forever loved everything prehistoric so it's no surprise when he chooses a dinosaur as a souvenir of his trip. Once home, he finds that his keepsake is more than he bargained for. No longer is the plastic figure just a toy. Sam keeps the dinosaur's powers to himself until his elderly neighbor accidently learns the secret. The young boy and the old man have much to learn about each other and their friendship helps both of them make some tough, life-changing decisions.

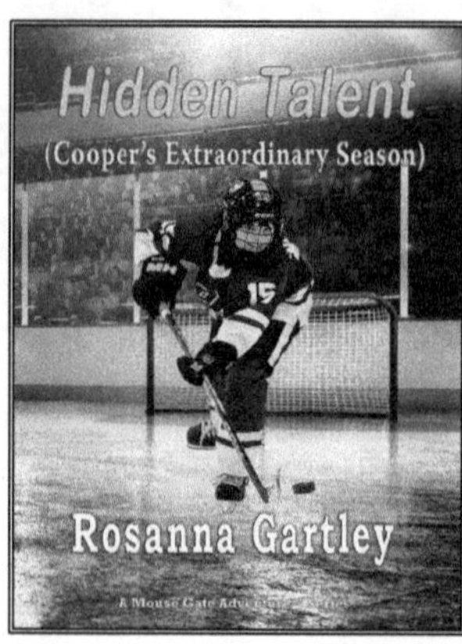

Title: *Hidden Talent*
 (Cooper's extraordinary season)
- Author: Dr. Rosanna Gartley
- Publisher: MouseGate.com
- Paper Back: ISBN: 9781648832147
- eBook: ISBN: 9781648832154
- Number of pages in the finished book: 96
- Publication Date: March 2025

Hockey is life! That's according to 12-year-old Cooper who has already spent 7 years playing the game. He is captain of his team and is in position to make a prestigious, elite team. But life takes an unexpected turn, showing everyone that he is much more than what they see on the ice.

Author's Bio

Dr. Rosanna Gartley is the mother of four adult children, four bonus adult children and grandmother to 15. A retired nurse practitioner, she currently lives in southwestern Pennsylvania but hails from the Canadian prairies. Rosanna enjoys her family, most things creative and travelling with her husband, John.

Mouse Gate Adventure Series Books
by Dr. Rosanna Gartley

This series of children's novellas are the perfect story time reads for boys and girls ages 8-12. For the younger child, they make excellent 'read to' books that often deal with everyday situations faced by children in the real world.

Each novella's tale contains action and adventure spurred by an issue or dilemma. Fantasy is sprinkled into the mix with the help of Disney Magic aiding the main character in solving the problem at hand. Rosanna's books not only entertain but educate as she weaves factual information throughout the engaging chapters.